Christine Pullein-Tho[...] [...]
horses all her life - she [...]
sisters when she was f[...]
fifteen and published [...]
Diana and Josephine. [...]
books which have been translated into eleven languages.
She is best known for her pony books but has also written the very successful Jessie series about a dog and
general fiction stories for younger readers. Christine
has four children and lives with her husband, Julian
Popescu, in a moated Parsonage with two horses, a dog
and a cat.

# HORSEHAVEN LIVES ON

**Christine Pullein-Thompson**

**CAVALIER PAPERBACKS**

© Christine Pullein-Thompson 1999

Published by Cavalier Paperbacks 1999
Burnham House
Jarvis St
Upavon
Wilts SN9 6DU

The right of Christine Pullein-Thompson to be identified as
the author of this work has been asserted by her in accord-
ance with the Copyright, Designs and Patents Act 1988

Cover illustration by Mark Smallman

ISBN  1-899470-09-3

Printed and bound in Great Britain by Cox & Wyman,
Reading, Berks

# CHAPTER ONE

## TURPIN IS RESCUED

We were on our way to rescue two dehydrated donkeys and a pony with sweet itch, just me, Cathy, Josh who is a little older than I am, and Jenny who owns and runs Horsehaven, a sanctuary for horses and ponies. We were in the Land Rover towing a trailer which contained haynets and headcollars as well as a twenty litre water container which only Josh could lift. It was bedded with straw.

"We'll water the donkeys first and give them hay if they need it, before we go on to look at the pony," Jenny said. The summer was ending; a huge sun was going down in the West. We passed a cloud of midges hovering over an almost empty pond. "The pony's tethered so that he can't scratch himself. Diabolical isn't it?" asked Jenny.

I imagined a pony standing on a tether unable to escape from the midges which consumed him. It wasn't a pleasant picture, and quite soon we reached two donkeys standing humbly by a gate. An old man on two sticks was waiting for us, smoking a pipe.

"Well done, you didn't take long," he said.

We dealt with the donkeys, lifting a padlocked gate off its hinges before filling a trough with water. There was plenty of grass in the field and tall trees to give shelter. Jenny checked the donkeys, picking up their hoofs and running her hand along their spines.

"They'll be all right for the time being," she told the old man. "But will you let us know if their owners are not back in twenty-four hours?"

She gave him our card as we watched the donkeys beginning to graze.

"They've been braying something awful. My neighbours have got more money than sense. They've been gone a week. I didn't bother for a day or two. I thought they had made arrangements," he said.

"Nothing, absolutely nothing surprises me any more," replied Jenny pushing her fair hair out of her eyes.

We left the old man still watching the donkeys and drove on.

"I wouldn't mind him as a Grandad," exclaimed Josh, before Jenny stopped to ask directions to a place called Brookley Green.

It was dusk now and a few minutes later we saw the reported pony walking round and round on a chain, his sides damp with sweat. There was no sign of water within his reach and it looked as though his tethering stake had not been moved for at least a day.

We leapt out of the Land Rover and saw that the top of his tail and most of his mane were rubbed raw. Worst of all there was a swarm of midges hanging over him, feeding in turn. I could feel tears pricking behind my eyes. I started to talk to him; but he didn't want conversation, he wanted to be free, to roll and gallop and above all scratch himself. Jenny and Josh opened a gate and ran towards a brilliant red front door in a house surrounded by an immaculate garden, the lawn good enough for a cricket match.

"I'm so glad you've come," said a woman appearing from the next house. "I was the person who rang you. He's been like this for days. I should have done something before, but my husband says one mustn't upset one's neighbour, you know what the Bible says, 'You must love your neighbours as you do yourself,' something like that anyway."

"I don't love myself much, so it wouldn't bother me," I replied.

"But why? You're so pretty," she said. "You must have loads of admirers."

I could see now that she was quite old and lived in another smarter world than I did. Then Jenny and Josh returned followed by a tall woman talking in a high pitched voice.

"My daughter will be back next week from working abroad and then she'll look after him. I'm not a horsey person and I'm just doing my best," she said.

The pony was too tormented to stand still. His fetlocks were swollen and his eyes only registered a wish to escape from his tormentors. He was black, a Fell pony, I thought.

"Either we take him with us, or I ring the RSPCA and the police, which means you are likely to be prosecuted for cruelty," Jenny said. I struggled to hold the pony who turned out to be called Turpin after the famous Highwayman, while Josh took incriminating photographs with the camera he takes everywhere with him. He took ten of Turpin and then some of the immaculate house and the well-maintained lawn which went with it. And I knew he was contrasting them - the poor pony and the opulent residence.

"You wait until these photos turn up in the local press and the reporters arrive here in droves, and everything is on TV," he said in a loud voice.

At the word, TV, the woman who was actually called Mrs Bell Smith began to shake. "Take him then. I don't want him. I was only keeping him for Alex. She loves him, she always has ever since she was ten years old."

"Funny sort of love," replied Josh before returning his camera to the Land Rover.

"Can you sign this form please?" asked Jenny. "It's to make everything legal. We don't wish to be accused of theft."

Once untethered, it took both me and Josh to hold Turpin.

"There's a water trough just inside the gate," Mrs Bell Smith said.

"He's quite a handful; I usually get the gardener or Mr Bell Smith to help me take him to the water. And I would have you know that I put calamine lotion on him twice a day and fly spray if he will stand still long enough."

After we had watered Turpin, Jenny threw down the ramp on the trailer and he rushed inside at the speed of an express train.

Mrs Bell Smith continued wittering on. "He and Alex were stars, they really were. I was only keeping him until she decided what she wanted done with him. 'Please keep him until I'm back, Mummy. If we have to sell him I want to thoroughly vet the home first,' that's what she said," Mrs Bell Smith continued. "We've got a lovely paddock, but he rubs himself raw on the fence. I've had the vet and he said it would be best to keep him on a tether. He gave me tablets, but I couldn't get him to swallow them. There is a loose box but it's stacked high with Alex's things and I daren't move them. I don't know what she'll say when she hears he's gone. I really don't."

In silence we put up the ramp on the trailer. Jenny fetched a pen from her bag and asked Mrs Bell Smith a second time, to sign along the dotted line of the form.

At that moment Mr Bell Smith appeared wearing bedroom slippers. "What's going on?" he asked in a plaintive voice before saying, "Look here, you can't take Alex's pony away. She'll never forgive us."

Watching Mrs Bell Smith sign the form, Jenny said, "Your daughter can visit Turpin any time, no problem."

"And we'll show her the photos when I've developed them. I've got a dark room at home, so it won't take long," added Josh cheerfully.

It was then that Mrs Bell Smith started shouting at her husband. "Don't just stand there George. Pull up the tethering stake. And what on earth are you doing out here in your bedroom slippers?"

Jenny thanked the woman who had reported Turpin's plight to us and was still hovering.

9

Mrs Bell Smith called after us, "I did my best, but I'm not one of you horsey women who know everything. I have other things to think of - my charity work, and keeping the house nice. They are the things which matter to me."

As we drove away Josh muttered something unrepeatable under his breath. Josh looks a softie with his wonderful fair hair and hazel eyes; but he isn't, he's tough, really tough, much tougher than I am. "You wait till I get my hands on Alex," he continued as Jenny changed gear.

"Maybe her mother doesn't tell her everything," I suggested.

"I bet she does or enough for her to know her pony's got sweet itch and is tethered," answered Josh.

"Some people don't have any imagination," suggested Jenny.

"But what about that other woman waiting weeks before she phoned us, with poor Turpin just outside her gate in agony?" I asked.

"People do that all the time and it's a terrible mistake. Never ever say to yourselves it's none of my business, it always is," replied Jenny vehemently driving on to a main road. "Report anything wrong and keep on reporting it," she continued, "and you might just save something dreadful happening to someone." Jenny was in a lecturing mood, for after that she told us the rules for humane tethering, how a pony should be tethered on a chain at least six metres long to a stake with a swivel on it, how there should be water available at all times, or the pony should be watered regularly, how the chain should be attached to a strap round the pony's neck and never to a headcollar, and that the stake should be moved daily. "There should be shelter too against wind and rain," she continued. "And in my opinion, no animal should be tethered for longer than twelve hours at a time, never night and day, and of course regular exercise should be provided, or a paddock where the poor animal can exercise itself."

When she paused for breath Josh said, "But it's not the law exactly, is it?"

"Only partly, because one must prove cruelty and if the pony looks fit and well, that's difficult. Sadly no court takes mental cruelty into account; but with your photos, Josh, we could easily prosecute the Bell Smiths, though I don't think I will because the stupid woman is never likely to have another pony, and it's just too much hassle."

"But it would be an example," I suggested.

"But still too much bother," repeated Jenny.

Since Jenny's partner Mark had disappeared, anything seemed to be too much bother for her - it was just one more thing to worry about.

It was nearly dark when we reached Horsehaven. I had left the puppy Jenny had just given me in a loose box because she wasn't house trained yet. I'd called her Vicky because she looked like a fox cub, a vixen, with a gingery red coat, and a gleaming white waistcoat. Now she threw herself at me, then ran in little circles of joy.

We put Turpin in a loose box bedded with shavings and gave him water and hay. Then Jenny threw a light summer sheet over him and said that we would call a vet in the morning. Turpin was much calmer now. As Jenny shut the stable door top and bottom to keep midges away he rested a hind leg and started to eat the hay.

I lived at Horsehaven, in the little room which long ago was the grooms' mess room, so I didn't need to go home. Instead I started to walk round the establishment for a last inspection, with tiny Vicky trying to keep up. First I looked at Hope and Faith, two Welsh cobs who had come to us through the RSPCA with matted coats and skeleton bodies. They were not old, but were prematurely aged by starvation and when you lifted their forelocks you found white hairs underneath and they had grey hair on their noses where their headcollars had become embedded. Their owners were being taken to Court. In the meantime we looked after them.

I inspected lop-eared Fantasy who had once been re-homed by us with disastrous results; and stringy, grey Trooper whom I loved best of all. Squid and Fidget, two short-legged, thick-necked ponies Jenny had bought from a market when Horsehaven was called Woodside and was still a riding school, ran their noses over me hoping for titbits. Tommy, a small ,Welsh liver chestnut, we had rescued from a life spent in a shed and chicken run was all right too. Bay Prince and palomino Goldie were lying down together, their poor misshapen hoofs tucked under them. The two other ponies, we had rescued at the same time as them, on a pouring wet night from a field sodden with rain, had already been re-homed. Sadly none of them would ever win best pony prizes with such terrible hoofs. Mystery and Secret, who belong to Barney Banks, a TV personality, were dozing standing up. Soon now they would be going to Ireland where he had bought a house. Then Regent, Mrs Sykes's dressage horse, would be our sole livery. I felt incredibly happy as I walked round the fields, because except for Fantasy who never put on any weight, all our animals were beginning to look better. Other than Turpin, Regent was the only horse stabled. This was because Mrs Sykes thought all animals should be kept in at night whatever the weather, (maybe she had never slept beneath the stars herself and discovered how wonderful and free it feels, or maybe like Alex she had no imagination). Poor Regent was fretting as usual longing to be out, his head over his box door staring anxiously towards the fields.

When I went indoors, Jenny's cat Charmer was lying on a chair in the kitchen and arched himself and spat at Vicky. "Watch it, he'll have Vicky's eyes out if you are not careful," Josh said drinking coffee and leaning against Jenny's old Raeburn cooker in her disordered kitchen, as though he lived there.

Next week we would start school again and I didn't want to go back. I didn't want to leave Vicky all day with Jenny. I wanted to stay with the horses at Horsehaven. They were my friends, the reason why I lived apart from my parents. I needed them as much as they needed me. Mum wanted me to be a nurse when I left school; but I had never felt the same way about people; maybe it was wrong of me, but that was how it had been for a long time.

Josh was phoning his mother now, who is separated from his Dad, saying, "I'm sorry I'm so late; it's been a busy day. But I'm leaving now."

Jenny started to cook supper. Her partner Mark was missing again. Anyone could see that their relationship was ending. I wasn't sorry, for he had never been a kindred spirit. He had hated his earnings being siphoned off to support a lot of horses he didn't care about and he had wanted Jenny to have an office job. Josh was leaving now muttering about school. He's a real boffin and plans to be a vet travelling the world rescuing horses. I think he will be. I think he can do anything if he sets his mind to it. But then I'm biased because Josh is the greatest guy I know and has been for a long time now.

"See you then," he said putting on his bicycle clips.

"Thank you for everything," replied Jenny. "I honestly don't know how we would manage without you."

"I'll get the photos developed as soon as poss," he said, going outside, shutting the back door after him as Jenny slid an omelette on to a plate and dished up peas to go with it.

Next morning a vet came, not the usual one but a red-haired woman who looked younger than Jenny. She slid a needle into Turpin's neck and left some ointment, and tablets to be mixed with his feed. Mrs Sykes had arrived by this time and was fussing over Regent, asking whether Josh would ride him for her because he was getting out of hand. She wears glasses and sees herself as a

14

great dressage rider. Next Bill, an ex builder, and our eldest helper arrived, and Gillian and Sarah who are both younger than I am. Everybody wanted to look at Turpin. Mrs Sykes kept on about him having lice, which just shows her ignorance because the effect of lice and sweet itch are entirely different. Gillian and Sarah groomed Turpin while Josh appeared and chatted up Mrs Sykes calling her "Mrs S."

It seemed like any other day at that moment, or rather better than most. Best of all Turpin was quiet now, the terrible itching had abated, his eyes were calm and his skin no longer twitched in torment. It seemed a shame that he had had to suffer for so long just because one woman cared more for her daughter, and another one didn't wish to quarrel with her neighbour. 'But what about the men?' I thought; their husbands? Why hadn't they done anything?

Later that day the old man rang to say that his neighbour had returned and that the donkeys were all right. That afternoon we lunged Goldie and Prince. Then Sarah the lightest and smallest of us gently mounted Goldie for the first time. One of us held the offside stirrup and then we waited holding our breath for something awful to happen. But Goldie wasn't bothered and feeling triumphant, Gillian led him round the covered school two or three times before Sarah dismounted to our most unhorsemanlike cheers. It was the same with Prince. "They don't mind because they see us as friends," Gillian said happily. It was another step taken towards them being re-homed, because we try to find our rescued horses suitable homes wherever possible, which is often incredibly difficult; for, as we've learnt through experience, people are not always what they seem. After what happened to Fantasy, he will remain with us forever; and so far, a home has not been found for Trooper. I love him so much that Jenny isn't hurrying to find him one, but I know one day that someone will want him as desperately as I do, and then he will have to go.

But Trooper was still with us on that September afternoon when Josh and I rode out together, Josh feeling like a king on beautifully schooled Regent, whom Mrs Sykes let him ride, though she wouldn't let me. And neither of us had an inkling then of what lay ahead as we cantered across fields of new stubble, imitating Mrs Bell Smith, and then imagining her daughter Alex, whom Josh said would be as thin as a beanpole with a loud voice and I said would have long dark hair and protruding teeth and a silly laugh. Regent went beautifully for Josh and Trooper had his ears forward and the swing in his stride told me that he was as happy as I was. I remember I wanted to go on riding for ever, but Josh insisted that he must see his mother before she went on night shift, so after an hour we turned back and cantered down a farm track with the sun in our eyes, side by side.

Turpin was turned out for an hour or two in the middle of the day when the midges went to wherever they go at that time. He was a different pony already. Gillian wanted to ride him, but Jenny insisted that she had to ask Alex or Mrs Bell Smith

16

first.

Turpin was in his loose box when we returned and I remember wanting life to stay the same for ever as I untacked Trooper and turned him out. Josh went home and I took Vicky for a walk as the sun set above the lime trees that line the drive. As I dawdled along waiting for Vicky to catch up, I remembered Horsehaven as it had been, the endless bills which had kept falling through the letterbox, bills we could not pay; the shortage of hay, the feed bins becoming emptier and emptier. Fantasy finding a home and then being sold on and how we had found him dying in a dreadful field between motorways. Since that day, none of us felt we would ever trust anyone again. Saving Tommy had been a nightmare too and there was still nothing to stop his owner Mr Reeves and his horrible daughter Selina reclaiming him.

There had been the terrible night when Vince and his drunken friends had let the horses out and Mrs Sykes's previous horse had had to be put down. And then there had been Rosa, a huge roan Shire whom Jenny had saved from an abattoir and whom we had all loved. Finally there had been the modelling I had done with some of our rescued horses for a shop's catalogue which had made enough money to settle all our bills. All this went through my mind as I walked with Vicky through the wood which goes with Horsehaven. It has a footpath through it and tall majestic beech trees and is thick with bluebells in the Spring and forever deep in centuries of fallen leaves, and I thought 'we are going to be all right now,' and I did not touch wood, though there was so much of it all around me. I thought of my Building Society account full of money, more than I had ever had before and soon I might be doing more modelling, and suddenly everything and anything seemed possible; even the start of school just two days away was bearable, and Vicky so small and puppyish was the best thing which had ever happened to me. But as Mum says, "After the sunshine comes the rain," and ordeals worse than rain were about to fall on us, but I didn't know it then; at that moment as far as I was concerned, life was all sunshine and there seemed no end to it.

# CHAPTER TWO

## JENNY GOES MISSING

Two days later Mark reappeared. I didn't see him but there must have been a terrible row between him and Jenny, because when I returned from school I found pieces of broken china all over the kitchen floor. When Vicky had stopped welcoming me with little squeaks of joy and much wriggling of her back end and many licks, I picked up the bits.

"I'm sorry. I regret throwing it at Mark now. It's my best Denby china and I loved it. But he just made me so angry," Jenny said, watching me.

"It's your house and it's your china," I replied fetching a dustpan and brush.

"I don't know what I saw in him, I really don't," continued Jenny beginning to cry. "He wants everything back that he gave us when this place was broke. He says it was only a loan."

I did not know what to say. I am not good at mopping up other's tears; "Was it a lot?" I asked after a moment putting away the dustpan and brush.

"According to Mark, it's several hundred pounds. I know he paid a whopping vet bill and the corn merchant. I thought his money was a gift. I thought he loved me," replied Jenny.

I wasn't surprised. It sounded typical of Mark,

whom I had never liked. Personally I had never seen what Jenny saw in him. He didn't even like animals. "You can have some of my money. I've got lots left from the modelling I did with Rosa and the ponies," I said.

"And Trooper too," said Jenny. "But no, thanks all the same Cathy. He can wait for it. We'll hold an Open Day and make some money that way."

"I don't think that's on, we are a bit short of horses and they will soon have their winter coats and the paddocks will be full of mud, and cars will stick in it. Anyway Mark won't sue you, will he?" I asked.

"You never know what Mark will do; he's totally unpredictable," replied Jenny. And I thought, she should know; because they had been partners for months and months, as long as I had known Jenny.

"And the vet bill for Turpin will be at least £100," continued Jenny in a dreadfully depressed voice.

"Can't Mrs Bell Smith pay it?" I asked.

"She wouldn't," said Jenny.

"How do you know she wouldn't?" I asked. We could send her Josh's photos and then she would be so frightened of them appearing in the press, she would pay anything."

"No. I won't blackmail anyone. I won't sink to it," replied Jenny. I made myself a mug full of coffee and tea for Jenny. School had been exhausting. We had a new teacher just out of college, who could not keep order and ostrich hamburgers for lunch; but I didn't eat them because I'm a veggie.

Drinking her tea, Jenny said, "There is some good news. Mrs Bell Smith rang to say that we could ride Turpin. She's expecting Alex back in a couple of days."

"Did she ask whether Turpin was better?"

"No nothing like that. She was extremely abrupt. She just said 'if it will help you, you can ride Turpin.' That was all," replied Jenny.

"And then rang off?" I asked.

Jenny nodded. I decided then that I would ring Mrs Bell Smith myself and demand that she pay Turpin's bill forthwith. Jenny, now so weak, suddenly made me feel strong and resolute. Mrs Bell Smith won't just walk over us, I thought, no way.

I was the only helper at Horsehaven that evening. I tacked up Turpin in an eggbutt snaffle and Trooper's saddle and rode him in the covered school. I thought he would be a quiet, comfortable ride, but he wasn't; he jogged and threw his head about. I decided that he was afraid of his mouth and as I rode, Alex went further and further down in my estimation. I rehearsed what I would say to Mrs Bell Smith on the telephone, deciding that if she were rude, I would simply slam down the receiver. Later when I had untacked Turpin, who although I had only ridden him for twenty minutes was sweating, an elderly person appeared in the yard driving an extremely ancient Mini. Jenny was tidying the muck heap, which we call the midden, which is something she does when she's suffering from stress. Putting down her fork she called, "What can we do for you?"

"I wondered whether you would have me as a helper here. I feel so useless and depressed living on my own. But there is one thing I know about

21

and that's horses. I used to have forty horses of my own you see," said the elderly person, getting out of her car. And immediately I thought, 'a know-all,' another Mrs Sykes but older and I made a face at Jenny which meant, 'No definitely not.'

But Jenny, the kindest person in the world, said, "We'll be honoured to have you. We need every extra helping hand we can get, old or young, Mrs..."

"I'm Alice Day. Lady Day actually, but please forget the Lady bit. Just call me Alice," she said looking at Jenny with fading blue eyes in a worn, leathery face framed by white hair and I remember thinking, she looks so ordinary, not like a titled person at all.

"Come inside and have a cup of tea and then I'll show you round. We haven't too many horses here at the moment," Jenny said.

"So you have a lot of empty beds, waiting for an emergency, just like a hospital," replied Alice laughing.

In spite of her slightly posh voice, the horses took to Alice straightaway. Even Fantasy, who is often nervous of strangers, rubbed his head against her, which until then he had only done to me.

Somehow that evening a new era seemed to start for us. I cannot explain it. Maybe it was Mark's behaviour which changed everything. Once again we needed money, just when we had hoped we had enough to see us through another year.

Later, when Jenny was out checking the horses for a last time, I rang Josh. I told him about Mark wanting his money back and about our new helper.

"We seem to be drifting back to square one. I really thought all our problems were over, but they seem to be starting up again," I complained.

Josh told me not to jump my fences before I came to them, (a horsey saying). He said that Alice sounded sweet and that Mark had been too mean to give Jenny much money so I need not worry.

"I expect he's lost his job and wants a new car," I replied bitterly. "You know what he's like."

"You are always gloom and doom, Cathy. Let's find out how much money is involved and take if from there," replied Josh sensibly. "We'll manage, we always have before."

"Until there's another crisis," I replied.

"There won't be one," answered Josh.

"Touch wood," I said.

When I had put down the receiver I went outside with Vicky and everything seemed very quiet and peaceful. Jenny was picking up muck in the fields. Turpin was standing in his loose box quietly munching hay in a hay net. His poor, scarred, tormented skin was healing. Before, his coat had been what horsey people call 'staring'; but it had changed and was becoming smooth and glossy. I wished humans could change as quickly. I wished he was a better ride as I stood there looking at him and I thought that somehow we had to improve him if we were ever to find him a home.

Returning indoors I looked up Mrs Bell Smith's number and feeling as though I had a pit in my stomach, rang it. A man answered in a gruff voice.

"Can I speak to Mrs Bell Smith please?" I asked.

Of course he wanted to know who it was, so after

a moment's hesitation I replied, "I'm speaking from Horsehaven."

"Well, I don't know whether she's around," he answered doubtfully, putting down the receiver.

A moment later Mrs Bell Smith asked, "Well, what is it now?"

"Turpin is doing very well," I said trying to sound like Jenny. "He's in all day, so the midges can't bite him and he's had an injection, tablets and ointment, and he isn't scratching any more." The pit in my stomach seemed to be growing larger every second. "We were just wondering whether you would settle the vet's bill if we sent it on to you," I said. And I thought, 'please God let her say yes.'

There was a long pause before Mrs Bell Smith said, "Why should I?"

"Because we are a very poor charity, and he is still your pony," I answered.

"He's Alex's pony. I'll let her decide. She'll be round to see you the day after tomorrow," and with that, Mrs Bell Smith rang off.

I felt better then, because as Mum says, if you don't do certain things you regret it later, and at least I had tried and though it wasn't very likely Alex would be all right, on the other hand she might be brilliant. She might not have known what was going on. And then I thought, it's good that Mark's gone, because he had been useless, he never really helped and I felt better. After that I went outside and chased Vicky round and round the stable yard until Jenny called, "Come in, it's supper time."

The next morning when I wandered out into the stable yard at seven o'clock I found Alice there, changing Regent's rug. She had already mucked him out and she looked thoroughly happy.

"Hello dear," she called, "I've done his stable. What can I do now?"

"Have you fed him?" I asked, "Because Mrs Sykes is very particular about what he eats."

"Yes, I checked the board in the tack room. I think he's getting too much. I think he should be turned out. He's so very highly strung and we don't want him to become a windsucker or a weaver," she replied laughing.

"Or a crib biter," I added wanting her to know that I knew something too.

"But Mrs Sykes likes him clean and tidy," I continued looking for a wheelbarrow.

"Don't you bother, I will see to Turpin," Alice called. "You get off to school. Go and have a good breakfast to set you up for the day."

I felt at a loss. I ran round the wood with Vicky. Then Jenny insisted that I ate a boiled egg for breakfast, while I told her about Alice.

"She won't get on with Mrs Sykes, that's for sure," I said. But Jenny said that she didn't need my opinion thank you and could I try to be a little more optimistic.

School dragged. I was glad when it was time to go home. Josh was in the top set for just about everything so I rarely saw him during school hours and he wasn't around when I left. Gillian and Sarah, our other helpers, go to a fee-paying school. There's a clique of girls in my class who have their

25

own ponies and go pony clubbing together, but I, never having a pony of my own, am not part of it. It started to rain as I left, pedalling away on my bike. It was Friday; it had been a short week because we hadn't gone back until Tuesday.

It was half past four when I reached Horsehaven and Turpin was still in the front paddock with midges attacking him from all sides. The Land Rover was missing. With a sinking heart I slipped a headcollar over Turpin's ears and after leading him into his box, shut the doors top and bottom for good measure. Then I ran into the house. Vicky was locked in my room and she had messed on the carpet. There was no message by the telephone and no Jenny. I looked around for smashed china, but there wasn't any. Everything was normal except that Turpin had been left out when the midges were at their worst and Jenny had disappeared.

Once, long ago when I was seven, I had returned from Primary School to what had seemed an empty house. I had looked for Mum and she wasn't there. I felt the same now. But then I had gone next door and found a neighbour and we had returned to the house together to find that Mum had been in the back garden all the time, and we had laughed our heads off. This time there was no neighbour to fetch; only Vicky gnawing at my school shoes and Charmer purring on the chair in the kitchen. I made myself a mug of coffee and it was then that I saw Jenny's message on the dresser: *Gone to rescue ponies at Newhouse Farm. Back soon - 2.15pm.* And looking out of the window I saw that the trailer had gone too. I hung about praying for the telephone to ring, but it stayed silent. At five o'clock I ran down to the end of the drive to see whether Jenny was returning, but there was no sign of her, so I dashed back to the house with Vicky snapping at my heels, and rang Josh.

"Jenny left at 2.15pm to rescue ponies and she isn't back," I said when he answered.

"That's not so very long ago," replied Josh, so calmly that I knew he was thinking, there Cathy goes, panicking again!

"But she left Turpin out to be consumed by midges and that's not like Jenny," I replied.

"We all make mistakes," answered Josh.

"Not that sort of mistake," I shouted back, "I know something's happened. Something awful. And where's Newhouse Farm?"

"Search me. I'll come over, ring Bill. But just make sure she isn't coming up the drive at the very moment I arrive or I'll scream." Josh put down the receiver.

I rang Bill. "Not to worry. I'll come over. I expect the Land Rover's broken down or she's had a puncture. Don't worry my darling, I will be with you in a jiffy." Bill put the receiver down before I had time to ask him about Newhouse Farm.

I wrote a note for Jenny and propped it up against the kettle. It said, *Gone to look for you. Will telephone every half hour if we can. Take care. Love Cathy.*

I went outside and looked down the drive. It was still empty. Bill and Josh arrived together. "She's at Newhouse Farm," I said.

"Where's that?" asked Bill while my heart went

27

down into my trainers and stayed there.

"I don't know. I thought you would," I cried.

"I don't know everything," replied Bill glumly.

"It can't be far away, or she would have put Turpin in the stable before she left," I answered.

Bill took a map from his truck. We pored over it. Rain was falling now and the sky was dark with more of the same. Suddenly, though it was still September, the summer seemed over. Josh saw the farm first on the map. "Look, it's only about ten miles away, let's go," he cried. "And leave Vicky behind because we don't know what we may find," he told me. "Go on, put her in your room."

I don't normally do what Josh tells me, but at that moment I felt too desperate to argue. Another minute and we were all in the front of Bill's old truck. It wasn't the first time we had searched for Jenny; on the last occasion she had been with Mark; this time she was alone which made it worse.

"She shouldn't go out on her own, it's asking for trouble," said Bill turning into the road. "She should have called me. I would have gone with her."

"What do you think has happened?" I asked.

"I don't know my darling," replied Bill.

"I expect she's all right. I expect we're being silly," Josh suggested. "After all Jenny isn't a child and she's not a fool either."

The roads were full of traffic. Bill's truck is nearly twenty years old and people kept hooting at him and making rude faces. Bill is almost bald with large capable hands and slightly bulging eyes.

Other than Jenny, he's the kindest person I know, and I have never known him lose his temper.

Looking at my gloomy face Josh said, "For goodness sake Cathy, everything is going to be all right," and he sounded like his mother, who is slim and efficient and used to dealing with emergencies.

But now Bill had stopped his truck at the corner to a lane where there was a large notice saying PRIVATE and another saying NO ADMITTANCE and further along a third saying, PRIVATE PROPERTY, and as we turned into the lane we saw to our dismay a fourth which said simply DANGEROUS DOGS. The atmosphere in the truck changed. Beads of sweat appeared on Bill's brow as he said, "This is it, and Jenny should never have turned down here. She should have gone back and fetched the police."

"Well you know Jenny and her 'hand to burn' attitude; her saying, that you must have a hand to burn for your country or a friend," said Josh.

"It doesn't apply any more, not when people use knives on each other; that saying belonged to the good old days," replied Bill, firmly changing into a lower gear. Bill seemed to be driving slower and slower now and his thick-veined hands looked shaky on the steering wheel and I had never known Bill frightened before. Soon we could hear dogs barking and I was glad I had left Vicky behind. Then we saw the Land Rover and trailer and I think at that moment all our blood ran cold. On the right of us was a hilly field and in it were white bones like toast racks, washed clean by rain.

"They're the carcasses of ponies," said Bill slowing

29

down, so that we could get a better view.

"You would think someone would have done something about it before now, wouldn't you?" asked Josh angrily.

"What, come down here past all those notices? You must be joking. It takes a fool like Jenny to venture here," said Bill bitterly.

"Not a fool, a hero," I argued. "She's the bravest person I know."

"That's fine up to a point," replied Bill. "But when others get dragged in and hurt, it's a different ball game."

We could see the farm house now covered with ivy and large, ferocious dogs frantically choking at the ends of chains. We came to yet another notice which read, KEEP OUT. PRIVATE PROPERTY. Inwardly I felt sick now with fear and disgust. "Where do you think she is?" I asked.

"That's anybody's guess." Bill had stopped calling me 'his darling.'

We reached a yard. Outside the truck the air was putrid. A few emaciated hens scratched feebly on a heap of rotting straw. A rusting tractor was parked in an open shed beneath a roof which had simply caved in. Five skinny kittens mewed piteously by a stable door asking to be let through.

"I think we should fetch the police," announced Bill switching off the engine of his truck.

"But what about Jenny?" I cried.

"Look, there are ponies over there and they are all skeletons. That's why she came," cried Josh before he leapt from the truck and started running across the yard calling, "Jenny where are you?

Jenny."

As I followed, Bill called, "Come back. Get back in my truck. Do you hear me, come back."

We ignored him. "He's afraid. He's an old man. He was in the Army when he was young and he couldn't take it," said Josh. "He told me all about it one day when it was raining and we were sitting in the tack room together. He fought in Malaysia after the real war was over. But we must find Jenny. We can sort out the ponies afterwards."

"Okay." Suddenly it was heart-lifting to be doing something; suddenly I wasn't afraid any more. Adrenalin rushed through me, like, I imagine, a quick fix must feel - not that I've ever tried one or wish to, I'm not that stupid. The chained dogs were hysterical with anger now, Rottweilers, razor thin, beautiful if you like the breed which I don't, salivating with rage. We looked in the Land Rover. There was Jenny's waxed jacket, Josh's camera and a pair of Wellington boots inside. The trailer had pony rugs in it, a bucket full of feed, headcollars, two hay nets. Josh found a broken shovel and picked it up. "It might come in handy," he said. (For a sworn pacifist Josh was becoming surprisingly warlike). "Look, there's an axe over there, grab it," he told me.

Bill was following us, looking all ways, bent double like a soldier on TV. Josh and I paused to look at three ponies in a small yard fenced by sagging wire. They looked as though they were dying on their feet. Tears welled in my eyes. "How can it have got like this without anyone doing anything?" I cried in anguish.

31

"That's obvious. No one's dared to come here," replied Josh before opening a shed door and looking inside, then calling, "Jenny, where are you?" in a desperate voice.

"Someone must have come to read the electricity meter," I said, "And someone must have told Jenny."

"You're joking. Look there are no wires. This farm isn't on anything. It's been left behind in a time warp. The owners must be crazy, or in need of special care," replied Josh.

I had been looking at the ponies. Suddenly I couldn't bear the sight of them a moment longer. I knew that their poor eyes looking at us without really seeing us, out of sunken sockets, would haunt me for ever.

"These are cases for the RSPCA, not us," grumbled Bill following us like a cross nurse. "Jenny should never have come here. She should have turned back when she saw the notices."

"What shall we do next? Search the buildings or knock on the back door?" I asked.

"You're not going near the dogs," replied Bill. "Do you hear me, you're to keep away from them."

It was at that moment we saw the rats, their small, brown, beady eyes shining in the dusk. They looked at us without fear; and they were everywhere, hundreds upon hundreds of them. A scream rose in my throat and died there. "Let's get back in my truck and go to the nearest house and call the police," said Bill glancing at us, his voice shaking. He was right of course.

But as we stood taut with horror staring at the

rats, trying to make up our minds to move, a man appeared. He was small and bearded, bent-backed with long matted grey hair and wearing split boots over sockless feet. He had a stick in one hand. He stopped to shout at the rats as though they were misbehaving dogs, and, looking at him, I cried, "We are looking for a friend. She called here a while back and her Land Rover's still here," and my heart thumped inside me like a sledge hammer gone mad, while my mind cried out, 'Flee Cathy, go on, run for it.'

But the man did not look at me. He looked at Bill. "Ain't I seen you somewhere before?" he asked through brown broken teeth. "Weren't we together at the end of the forties? Ain't you called Bill?"

"And you are Dave," replied Bill. "What a surprise," and standing in that dreadful yard with the rats watching us like an audience in the theatre, they shook hands like old comrades.

# CHAPTER THREE

## TWO FOALS AND A
## POOR LITTLE MARE

"My mother says you can judge someone by his friends," said Josh staring at Bill. "I just wonder where they met."

"As soldiers of course," I replied quickly, just as Bill turned towards us to call, "Jenny's in the wash house. If you go round the side of the house, the dogs won't get you."

We kept our weapons and ran. There was a little path at the side of the house and a dreadful smell of rotting refuse. An old woman's face, pinched and dirty, wearing glasses and framed by long unkempt hair, stared at us through dusty leaded window panes and her eyes became horribly like those of a scared rabbit as we watched. There was a little yard at the back of the house, with outbuildings - a loo, a coal shed, and one in the middle with a locked door, or so it seemed at first, until Josh observed it was simply bolted top and bottom, and all the time while we looked, I was afraid that the dogs might break their chains and tear us to pieces. Then Josh shot back the bolts and the door was open and Jenny was throwing her arms around our necks crying, "I thought I would never get out. I really thought it was the end because there are no visitors here - it's a madhouse," she continued.

"You should have waited for us to come with you," said Josh sternly.

"Somebody telephoned from a hot air balloon up in the sky. He could see everything. I don't know how he knew our number. He should have rung the police," Jenny said, stepping outside, before adding, "We've still got work to do. But how did you get here? How on earth did you find this place?"

"It was on Bill's map; he brought us and he knows the man here, it's really scary," I told her, but now suddenly I wasn't afraid any more.

"Look, they are talking like old friends," added Josh pointing. And it was true; they were standing together like two real buddies swapping stories.

"That's better than fighting," said Jenny. "But listen, there are two foals which we can rescue and a poor little mare who is trying to feed them both; she is so emaciated she can barely stand. Come on. They are Shetlands and really small."

I told Jenny about the other ponies we had seen, but she said that they were stallions and probably past the point of return. I threw down my axe and Josh, being tidier, leant his broken shovel against a wall.

The foals were in a small dark stable behind the other buildings. There were two mares with them, but one was dead. I felt empty inside.

"We'll carry one foal first, then go back for the older one and the mare," said Jenny, in a deadpan voice.

The smallest foal must have been no more than two days old. Josh carried her head and I carried her quarters, while Jenny opened the trailer. Bill and Dave had gone into the house and suddenly, quite unexpectedly, the dogs had stopped barking. We lay the foal down in one part of the trailer and I stayed there while Jenny and Josh went back for the others. The other foal managed to stagger up the ramp but we had to help the mare. Once inside, she nosed the hay net and then started to eat very slowly, like someone with toothache.

"That's a good sign. We may be just in time," said Jenny. "But I don't think she can have much milk left."

A few moments later we were leaving that dreadful yard. "Are you sure we can't save any of the others?" I asked.

"I don't think so, but it needs a vet to decide," Jenny replied and I saw then how tired she was with dark circles under her eyes and her hair all over her face. "That dreadful crazy man put a scarf over my eyes; I thought he was going to strangle me. I was just so frightened," she said.

And I didn't know what to say. We had reached the road now. "It was really scary finding you weren't at home. I knew something awful had happened," I said presently.

"Whatever happens next, however poor we are, I'm going to buy a mobile phone," Jenny said, changing gear. "Then I can phone for help if I need it, and I certainly needed it today. I just can't tell you how awful the chicken houses are, with corpses lying in battery cages and eggs still rolling along underneath them, and the smell. I'll never forget it."

"There's a telephone kiosk. Look over there. Stop,"

cried Josh. He and I had a look at the Shetlands while Jenny telephoned the police and the RSPCA. The mare was still nibbling at the hay. The two foals lay stretched out, their faces so tiny and sweet, their little tails like foxes' brushes. They were both dark brown, almost black, and they too smelt dreadful. We could see lice clustered around their tiny ears, sucking and sucking, their mouths embedded in the foals' flesh.

"I've rung the police and they'll be contacting the RSPCA," Jenny said climbing back into the Land Rover.

"But what about Bill? We just drove out and left him," I said.

"He's old enough to look after himself. Anyway you know the saying, 'Old Soldiers never die.' He'll be all right Cathy, I just know he will," replied Jenny while Josh said, "I think this has been the most nauseating rescue of them all. I can't imagine how such a place can exist among us. It makes one think doesn't it?"

"I don't think there's any end to cruelty," replied Jenny slowly. "We are lucky that we can do something about it, that we have police who care and a society which can help, and yet it still happens, animals still starve to death, badger baiting still goes on, illegal traps are still set and hens rot in battery cages."

"But at least we don't beat dogs to death before we eat them, or make skeleton horses pull carts in cities in harness which rubs them raw. At least most of it is underground and unseen. Is that what you mean?" asked Josh.

"I suppose so, but sadly it is still here and we are supposed to be civilised," replied Jenny.

"And it shouldn't happen, not ever," I cried. "Not here or anywhere else. It should never ever be allowed."

"But how come the balloonist knew our address? And our telephone number?" Josh asked.

And then Jenny replied, "I remember now, he said he had a girl called Samantha with him who had come up for the ride."

"Samantha?" I cried.

"Good old Sammy," said Josh beginning to laugh.

I imagined Samantha in a hot air balloon, her luscious hair, her perfect skin. Her horse had died of ragwort poisoning. She had been a helper, but a half-hearted one. Josh had liked Samantha. I had had a bet with her which I had won. Her father had suddenly been declared bankrupt and they had all gone to London. I had been glad to see Samantha go.

"She's still making amends for her horse dying," Jenny said.

"That's unfair," Josh replied. "She was simply doing what comes naturally and thank goodness she remembered our number."

"If only she had rung later, we could have assembled a proper team," I suggested. But we all knew that wasn't Sammy's way of doing things; she couldn't wait for anything. We fell silent. It was twilight, an early autumn twilight. The rain had stopped. And then at last we saw the lights of home shining out like a beacon.

"Oh Cathy, did you put them on?" cried Jenny

38

sounded exasperated, no doubt already lamenting the expense.

"Of course I didn't. I'm not a complete idiot. Anyway it was light when we left," I retorted. "There are probably vandals there, tearing the place to pieces."

And then Jenny put her foot down so hard on the accelerator that the Land Rover shook, but there were no vandals, only Alice cheerily skipping out. "I think I've done everything," she called, in a voice surprisingly young for one so old. "I've walked Vicky too and put the kettle on."

Jenny stopped the Land Rover and switched off the engine.

"There was only one call from someone called Alex, who is coming at around ten o'clock tomorrow to look at Turpin. That doesn't mean he's homed already does it?" asked Alice.

Jenny, who had told her about Alex several times already, sighed, but Josh jumped out of the Land Rover and ran across the yard to embrace her crying, "Oh Alice you're wonderful, really wonderful."

Alice looked flustered, but happy, as I climbed down from the Land Rover. "Vicky was ever so good; she really is a lovely little dog, a real gem," she said.

There was a loose box bedded down waiting for an emergency. We carried the foals into it, while the mare followed hobbling uncertainly on hoofs so long that it was a wonder she could walk at all.

"Oh how dreadful. How absolutely dreadful!" cried Alice.

"I'm going to ring the vet; they need bottle feeding," said Jenny.

"Unless we can find a mare which has lost its foal," replied Alice.

"Which will be like looking for a needle in a hay stack," said Jenny.

"And if they don't get fed, it's curtains for them, anyone can see that," said Josh.

The vet, that Jenny spoke to, advised her to go to a stud farm twenty miles away, insisting that they had the right equipment there and they would help.

"It's a Friday night. I expect he's planned an evening out," said Alice, alluding to the vet.

"We owe them a lot of money," replied Jenny, getting back into the Land Rover. "So I don't suppose they want to come here again." Josh went with Jenny. I stayed. I mixed the Shetland mare a small feed, and looking at her poor misshapen hoofs, burst into tears. I fetched her water and put glucose in it and saw that she had bald patches all over her caused by malnutrition. I would have liked to put my arms around her and weep into her matted coat, but she smelt too bad and had lice all over her. I found myself washing my hands after I had touched her, while Alice made us both coffee.

A little later the vet rang. "Good news," he said in a loud cheerful voice. "I've found a little mare who has loads of milk. My colleague was called out to her yesterday. It's a strange case. She's thirty years old and she hasn't a foal, but she's running with it, literally. I've told her owners to bring her straight over to you."

"Brilliant," I cried. "But I hope she's really small because the foals are absolutely tiny."

"You'll have to stand them on boxes then won't you?" laughed the vet. "No she's a Dartmoor, a little one, so don't fret. I expect it will be all right."

"Thanks a million," I replied but he had already rung off.

"Someone's bringing a mare with milk," I cried. "Everything's going to be all right. Poor Jenny and Josh, they needn't have gone to the racing stables after all."

"But she may not bond with them. Motherhood is a funny thing," replied Alice, whom I saw now for the first time was at least five centimetres smaller than I was. "So we may need bottled milk after all."

Ten minutes later a horsebox stopped in the yard. A woman and a girl leapt out. "We brought Beechnut over straightaway; we know she would love to be suckling foals, she's frightfully maternal," said the girl, who was probably my age with long hair in a pony tail, while her mother had short straight hair and a squarish face. We showed them the Shetlands and the girl said straightaway, "But what's wrong with them? I mean supposing they have some dreadful disease. And look at their lice. We don't want Beechnut to catch anything. She taught me to ride."

"And she is very old," echoed her mother.

"They are suffering from starvation," I said slowly. "But if you would rather take Beechnut away again, please do. We don't want to be blamed for anything, do we Alice?" Suddenly I was glad to have Alice with me.

"Certainly not. And we are going to delouse them immediately," said Alice.

The girl was called Lisa and she and her mother now knelt in the straw and looked at the foals and the poor starved mare. "She hasn't a drop of milk left, just feel her udder," Lisa said.

"Shall we risk it?" asked the mother, while Alice and I waited in suspense.

"They'll be dead by morning if we don't," replied Lisa.

"We'll risk it then," decided her mother.

We made a pen for the Shetland mare out of bales of straw and led Beechnut into the loose box. Alice and I stood the foals up and introduced them to their new mother. We fed her pony nuts and talked to her, but it was half an hour before the foals were sucking properly; by that time Jenny had arrived back and Josh had gone home.

"I think it's going to be all right," said Lisa.

"Finding you here was such a wonderful surprise. I don't know how to thank you," said Jenny to Lisa and her mother.

"Don't. We're doing it for the same reason as you are," replied Lisa before joining her mother in the cab of the horsebox.

"Well a million thanks just the same," I said, while Jenny called, "We'll ring you tomorrow," her exhausted face crinkling into a lopsided smile. Alice was already sitting in the kitchen, looking exhausted, when we went indoors. Jenny offered to take her home, but she said that she would be all right in a minute and could drive herself. Night had come to us unnoticed. Already my day at school seemed to belong to another age.

"I think they are going to be all right. I think we've saved them," Jenny said.

"But not the others, not the skeletons in the fields and those poor stallions and all the hens," I replied slowly, remembering.

"We are not God, we can only do our best," Jenny replied, before the phone rang. It was Mark. During the next few days he would ring frequently demanding his money back, driving Jenny to despair. But eventually Jenny put down the receiver and Alice went home and we had supper.

Twice that night Jenny and I returned to the stable to check on the Shetlands; both times we were overwhelmed by the feeling of contentment which now existed among them all. Beechnut had taken to the foals; the Shetland mare was lying down in her pen looking at peace with the world.

"Every time I look at them, I feel all gooey inside," I said.

"Same here," agreed Jenny. "Just the sight of them makes me feel happy; it helps me realise how little money really counts and yet when you haven't any you're helpless; it's almost like being in prison."

"Don't think of it. Mark won't sue," I replied quickly.

Shutting the loose box door after us, Jenny said, "You must be kidding; he's given me just two weeks to pay the £350 he says I owe him, or else he's taking me to Court, and that won't do this place any good. It's diabolical; he's skint as usual and he's taking it out on me." We washed our hands again at the kitchen sink. Then Jenny made us both tea and now it was past midnight. No school tomorrow, I thought and on Sunday I will catch the bus to Westcliffe-on-Sea and see Mum and Dad. I'll take Vicky with me. She'll love the sea. I saw myself eating home-made cake and telling Mum about the foals and Newhouse Farm. Away from it all, I might be able to laugh again and Dad would be interested in Dave and Bill because his Dad had also fought in Malaysia all those years ago. But at that moment as I climbed into bed I felt more like tears than laughter.

# CHAPTER FOUR

## VISITING THE RIDING SCHOOL

That night I dreamt Mark returned. "Either pay up or I'll destroy this place," he cried. "And I'll make sure it's all over the tabloids. OWNER NOT FIT TO RUN HORSE SANCTUARY, and that will be the end of it once and for all. You can sell up then, Jenny and pay me back what I lent you, with interest."

A minute later, while I was still gasping with horror, Sammy arrived on the scene. "Don't worry Jenny. I'll pay. I've brought the money," she said, throwing her arms around Jenny and kissing her. "It's what I earned working on the till at Tesco's in Westcliffe-on-Sea. You can have it all."

Josh appeared then and, kissing Sammy, cried, "Oh you're brilliant, absolutely brilliant. I always knew you were, not like poor old Cathy who never has two pennies to rub together."

I woke up then and was sure that the dream had been some sort of omen, because of the money I still had in my account from the modelling I had done. I was certain now that I must give it to Jenny. I got up and dressed; it was half past six and the foals were standing up in their loose box looking sweet, while the Shetland mare ate hay as though she would never stop and Beechnut stood trying to look over the loose box door. (She was too small to put her head over it). Vicky ran round and round the yard in mad circles and I could see the sun breaking through clouds, and everything was still and beautiful and empty with the leaves on the trees, yellow, green, russet and gold. And I thought, 'whatever happens in the future I will always love this place more than anywhere else on earth.' I fed Regent, who was banging on his door as usual, and Turpin who was still coming in at night; then I walked across the fields to look at the others. Hope and Faith were lying down; Fantasy and Trooper were grazing together, as were Star and Goldie; only Tommy seemed to be alone, for Fidget and Squid were standing nose to tail by their field gate like old friends. And I saw that the fields were full of mushrooms, and I picked a bucketful; wandering about, I felt as though Horsehaven was mine.

A few minutes later Alice arrived and called, "You've beaten me to it. I couldn't sleep a wink. I was awake all night worrying about the foals. Are they still with us?"

"They're fine," I said, thinking that she looked old, too old to work as hard as she did. But oblivious of her age, she fetched a wheelbarrow and said briskly, "I'll start with Regent." She was wearing incredibly ancient clothes; she always did. She said she bought everything she needed at charity shops. "There's no need to spend £90 on an overcoat when you may kick the bucket next week," she had said, laughing as though life was just a joy ride which you suddenly got off. And the horses loved her, a little more each time she came to help. They never pushed her rudely or trod on her feet.

"Alice, Mrs Sykes is supposed to muck out Regent. He's a do-it-yourself livery," I told her now. "Why don't you go inside and have a nice cup of tea?" But she only laughed.

Hope and Faith were still having feeds every day, full of garlic and vitamins. When I arrived with their two feed buckets, they galloped across what we call the long paddock, to meet me. They were typical Welsh cobs, except that they were still so thin that they looked ewe-necked and sickle-hocked. But at least their coats were beginning to grow over the dreadful bald patches, which were interspersed with their matted hair, which was beginning to fall out. And the fact that they could gallop was a step forward. Fantasy and Trooper had feeds too; but the ponies were living on grass for a while longer. It was now like any other day, except that my dream hung over me like a question mark, for half of me wanted to give my money to Jenny while the other half said, 'it's all you've got and you earned it.'

Jenny and I were eating a hurried breakfast when Bill appeared. He came straight into the kitchen and sat down heavily on the kitchen stool, the one he always uses. He looked shattered. 'Shell shocked,' Jenny was to say later. "You're all right then? You've got over your ordeal then?" he said, looking at Jenny. Nodding, Jenny continued eating toast. "He was my mate," continued Bill. "He saved my life. And now they're taking away everything on the farm, burning carcasses, destroying chickens, everything's diseased apparently."

"Do you mean the police?" asked Jenny pouring him tea, and heaping sugar into it.

"The RSPCA, the police, the Social Services. It doesn't really matter, does it? They've even taken the old lady away. They want to burn the place down."

I remembered the rats, the skeleton ponies staring at us with hopeless eyes, the dead mare. I got up and threw my tea down the sink and gave my remaining toast to Vicky.

"We went through the war together in Malaysia," Bill continued. "He saved my life."

"So did my grandad. He went through it, but it's an awfully long time ago. He died when I was two, but I can still remember him ... just," I said.

"You really started something when you went there, Jenny," Bill continued, ignoring me. "You set the wheels in motion."

"You didn't see the chicken houses, Bill. It should never have got that far. What I saw will haunt me for ever and I can't forgive; I'm sorry, Bill," replied Jenny. "And would you like to be locked in a shed, Bill? I could sue your Dave, take him to Court, have him locked up, but I won't because you knew him Bill, because he saved your life."

"The foals are covered with lice," I said to break a silence, which was suddenly heart rending. "They matter too Bill." I went outside into the air, which now seemed extraordinarily fresh, where there was the lovely smell of healthy horses, of hay, of saddle soap and horse feed.

By nine o'clock the yard was full of people. Gillian and Sarah arrived first, closely followed by Josh on his mountain bike. Gillian and Sarah were determined to work on Goldie and Prince and went straight to their field to collect them. Josh started to groom Regent. (He helps Mrs Sykes and then she lets him ride Regent as a reward). Next Miles appeared with his mother and little sister Amy. Miles's wheelchair was pushed into the room next to the kitchen, where Jenny has an office. He had brought a bag full of discs and his computer and started working on Horsehaven's accounts straightaway while Amy rushed round the yard pretending to be a bucking bronco. I was just about to turn Turpin into one of the fields, when a small dumpy woman with hair wound into a plait round her head appeared. I couldn't think who she was until she held out a hand saying, "I'm Alex, Turpin's owner." She was so different to what I had imagined that my mouth must have fallen open with surprise, for the next thing she said was, "What's the matter? Weren't you expecting me?" and gazed at me with such quiet brown eyes that I couldn't imagine her ever getting unnerved or cross.

"Nothing, absolutely nothing. Of course we're expecting you. I'm Cathy. Hi," I said.

"I've brought a cheque for you. I managed to squeeze it out of my mother," continued Alex handing her a white envelope. "It's for the vet."

I thanked her profusely, before taking her to see Turpin, who whinnied to both of us.

Alex said that her parents needed stringing up. They had had their instructions and they didn't keep to them. She said that she had only been away three months and Turpin had had a stable and a field, and occasional tethering if necessary. She said that her parents had called a vet, who only understood cows and had probably never seen a horse before and, as she talked, I began to like her more and more.

"You are not going to prosecute Mother are you?" she finished.

"It's not in my hands, but I doubt it," I said.

I took Alex indoors to see the photos Josh had taken of Turpin the day we rescued him. She put on a pair of wire glasses and stared at them, before crying, "Oh Mother is just so stupid. Didn't she think? Poor Turpin, he looks so awful. Couldn't she see how he looked? Honestly, she must be mad or something."

"I expect she did what she thought was right," suggested Jenny, appearing. "I expect she thought the vet must know everything, and like everyone else, vets come good and bad ...Anyway, we are not going to prosecute. What do you want us to do with Turpin, Alex?"

"Find him a good home. I'm going to be working in London for a tiny wage. I shall probably begin in Harrod's like all my friends, probably down-stairs doing the packing. I can't stay at home," replied Alex. "But I've got some savings so I'll send you some money for Turpin's keep and you can ride him as much as you like - I just don't want his sweet itch to come back."

"We know a riding school by the sea, where there are no midges. It's a very happy place and it might suit Turpin," said Jenny.

"And you could visit him whenever you liked, you could even ride him there," I added hopefully. "I shall probably go there tomorrow. You can come with me if you like," I suggested.

Alex said she would take me there in her car. Then we went round the fields together, before she left, and suddenly, without real reason, there seemed hope on the horizon. I know we all felt uplifted by her visit. Of course I still had to explain the cheque to Jenny who, when I gave it to her, said, "I am so very grateful to you, Cathy, but please don't pretend to be me ever again. It could cause terrible trouble. I know you rang them because their number is on my telephone account."

"I didn't say who it was speaking, I let Mrs Bell Smith make up her own mind," I retorted. "She could have asked and then I would have said. I didn't lie." But Jenny lectured me all the same, saying that because we were a Charity ,we had to be whiter than white and the first thing you should say when you start a telephone conversation is who you are. I thought Jenny was being very ungrateful but I didn't say so. Until now she had always been my heroine, absolutely and beyond all possible doubt. Now she had slipped a little.

I said, "You're taking it out on me because you're upset over Mark." Then I went outside, slamming the back door after me. I found Mrs Sykes and Alice quarrelling.

"I know you understand more about horses than the rest of us will ever learn, but Regent happens to be my horse and a very expensive one too, and how I treat him is my business Alice. Is that quite

51

clear?" Mrs Sykes was saying.

"I still think he needs more time out and I will till I die," replied Alice stubbornly.

To stop them quarrelling, I said, "There are lots of mushrooms in the fields, would you like some?" But neither answered, so I left them to it and found Sarah and Gillian in the covered school riding Goldie and Prince, with Josh in the middle shouting instructions. Both ponies were going beautifully and now I wished that I was ten again like Sarah and just as carefree. Amy was sitting on an upside down bucket watching. "We're going to ride Squid and Fidget next. Josh is teaching us," called Sarah happily. And now I was glad that I was visiting my parents the next day at the caravan site Dad manages. I wanted to go to the Sea Top Riding School again, for suddenly I felt a desperate need to get away from the squabbles and the many problems at Horsehaven.

The next morning Alex picked me up in her car, and drove carefully and slowly with Vicky wildly excited in the back. "Mother lent Turpin to a dreadful girl called Tracey when I was away. She was supposed to look after him in exchange for riding. But do you know what she did? She tied him to a tree in a garden while she visited her boyfriend, and after two hours, Turpin escaped and galloped along a main road and caused two cars to run into each other before he ended up upside down in a pub car park. Just imagine it!" Alex exclaimed. "And all without my permission. That's my mother for you, Cathy."

"What about your father?"

"He keeps out of her way; he only potters about in the garden; and once he was an important bank manager," lamented Alex.

So it was probably the girl called Tracey who had ruined Turpin's mouth, I thought, not Alex. And seeming to read my thoughts, Alex said, "Tracey couldn't ride. My mother must have been stark staring bonkers to lend him to her." Next Alex told me that she had been teaching English to foreigners abroad, in Turkey of all places, she said, and that it had been a nightmare, and now we could see the sea gently washing pale golden sand.

I told her about my parents. "You won't like them, they're not smart," I said, "Just ordinary." After that I explained why I lived at Horsehaven, how they had moved and how I couldn't bear to leave the horses and Jenny. "But I do miss them sometimes," I added.

Alex asked me whether I intended to go to college and I said that I was trying and hoping, but that I might not be clever enough and then we were driving into the caravan site and Dad was waving like mad and calling, "Cathy's here. She's arrived," and my mother rushed out into the garden, laughing, while Vicky went mad with excitement in the back of the car.

"What a welcome. What lovely parents," said Alex, stopping the car. We ate a veggie lunch, sitting outside in the sunshine while Vicky played with a ball and happy holiday makers shrieked around us. Then we walked through the sand dunes to the Sea Top Riding School. As usual the

53

yard was in chaos, bikes flung down, wisps of hay scattered across concrete. We found the proprietors, Les and Suzie, with mugs of coffee in their hands. They put them down to embrace me. A moment later, I was introducing Alex and telling them about Turpin. Then I rushed to see the two ponies they had on loan from us, cuddly roan Rowan and sturdier bay Star.

"They are great favourites here," Suzie said.

"They're shaping up really well," added Les, "But the farrier can't get their hoofs right. I don't think they ever will be right, but we'll keep on trying."

I told Les and Suzie how well Goldie and Prince were going, while Alex wandered round the yard, not saying a lot, until Les told us that they must get on, because the afternoon ride would be going out in twenty minutes, but that they would like Turpin if we felt they were suitable, and that because of the breeze from the sea, midges were not a problem.

"What do you think?" I asked Alex, as we walked back across the sand dunes, while Vicky ran ahead stopping constantly to dig in the sand. "Do you want them to have him?" I asked.

"Yes, if Jenny agrees."

Dogs were not allowed on the beach, so Mum looked after Vicky, while we wandered down to the sea. Then Alex said she must get back and Mum handed me a bag full of food: home-made cakes, bananas, bars of chocolate, saying as usual, "You look half starved, Cath," to which I replied, "I like looking that way."

Driving home, Alex and I ate the chocolate and I

told her about Les and Suzie, how well they ran the riding school, how any horses working more than three hours a day, rested on the next one, and she said that Turpin used to love work and that he had been tireless, but that Fells were like that, weren't they? I remembered that they had been bred as pack ponies to bring roofing slates down from Northern hills and Alex said, "And to work on little hilly farms." And then we were back at Horsehaven again.

"Hi there," called Jenny. "I've got lots of news. First of all we've got a show jumper which needed homing. Come and look."

We followed her to where a 17 hand horse looked at us over a loose box door. He had a trickle of white down his face and patting him, I thought, he'll need an awful lot of feeding. "Someone found him neglected in a field," Jenny explained, "And persuaded his owner to send him here. Once the poor fellow jumped for England. He won too, apparently; it was the year the British Team won in Germany. It was before your time, Cathy," she added. "Anyway nowadays he's known as Torchy, short for Night-Time Torchlight."

"And the other news?" I asked.

"Samantha's back, she and Josh have gone off somewhere. And Vince has been here looking for you."

"Why did Sammy come back here?" I asked.

"Because she wanted to of course. She's staying with friends," replied Jenny laughing.

I had tried to like Sammy. She was outgoing and fun, but had always skived off, when the work

55

became hard. We all knew it. Yet Jenny and Josh still liked her, didn't seem to notice that I had worked much harder than she did. Somehow Sammy's hands had always remained clean, and her clothes had always had trendy labels on them; but worst of all Josh had been my friend until Sammy came along. As for Vince, he had been her boyfriend, until she had chucked him for Josh. Vince had blamed Horsehaven and had appeared one night with friends and let all the horses out with heart-rending results, and now he wanted me to go with him! "He must be mad! I don't want ever to see him, and why isn't he in prison?" I asked.

"He did his community service and paid a fine, now he says he's a reformed character," Jenny told me. "I'm sorry he called. I told him you weren't interested but he won't be put off."

"I don't want to speak to him. Okay? Not ever."

The day was ruined now. I said goodbye to Alex. I told Jenny that Les and Suzie wanted to have Turpin and that Star and Rowan were fine. And all the time there was a knob of fear growing inside me, that wouldn't go away. I had always disliked Vince, he knew that. I had made it so plain to him.

"Don't look so glum, Vince can't make you go out with him," Jenny said laughing. "Come in and have some tea." But now I didn't think I would ever want to eat again. I wished that I hadn't come back from Westcliffe-on-Sea, that I lived there. I didn't want to face Vince and I didn't want to see Sammy and Josh together again.

# CHAPTER FIVE

## TOMMY GOES

I was late for school the next day. I had risen early enough; but Alice was in the yard before me, looking like a scruffy mouse in an old grey duffel coat, brown cords and Wellies. She had the wheelbarrow, the best shovel, ditto broom and fork and, when I needed to fill a bucket with water, she always seemed to be at the yard tap, running the water so slowly that I wanted to scream. And I was used to having it all my own way in the morning. I had always enjoyed the horses' heads looking over stable doors expectantly, their glad whinnies when they saw me. Now Alice had stolen those lovely moments from me and there was nothing I could do about it. I know I wasn't very nice about it and poor Alice kept saying things like, "I won't be a minute dear, just be patient." But to someone in a hurry, Alice's minutes sometimes seemed like hours.

When I eventually arrived at school there was hay in my hair and I realised that I had forgotten to eat breakfast. Without thinking, I shook my head and the hay fell out on to the classroom floor, which caused a lot of amusement.

It had been a bad morning for Jenny too, with Mark on the telephone at seven o'clock and heaps of nasty brown envelopes containing final demands for bills to be settled, dropping through the letterbox. Worse than that, Tommy's owner had rung to say that he had found a field for his little girl's pony and wanted him back, adding that Selina had had riding lessons and would be able to look after him properly. And of course, when she told me this, I remembered rescuing Tommy - the tiny shed without any bedding, which was his stable, the small chicken run fenced by wire netting without a blade of grass in it which was his field. Worse still, I had grown fond of liver chestnut Tommy and we all knew how happy he was with us. "I just hope the field is bigger than the last one," I said.

"They are arriving this very evening," Jenny continued. "They are going to pay for his keep while he was here - cash."

"Brilliant, but make sure you add on the worm doses he's had," I answered. This had all happened between seven and eight in the morning. Afterwards school was a disaster. First there was the hay on the floor, then I bumped into Josh in break. He's a real boffin and had the usual book under his arm. But he wasn't reading it, or thinking about it, for the first thing that he said was, "Have you heard, Sammy's back?"

"Yeah, sure, big deal," I lied, trying to sound offhand.

"And she hasn't changed a bit," Josh laughed again.

"Great," I replied while my heart sank into the boring black shoes I wear to school. "Is she going to help then?" I asked.

"I doubt it. She never was one for work was she?" replied Josh indulgently. When I returned to Horsehaven, Les and Suzie were loading Turpin into their trailer. "Hi Cathy, well done," Les called to me. "Turpin's just what we need because he'll take light adults as well as children and one of our 14.2s has gone lame."

"But you haven't tried him," I cried.

"Don't worry, he'll be all right," Suzie said.

I didn't mind Turpin going. He had never been a particular favourite of mine, not as Trooper and Fantasy were and for a short while the Shire mare, Rosa, who had found a super home recently as a brood mare. Watching Tommy go would of course be different.

Jenny and I waved goodbye to Les and Suzie before we went indoors. Handing me a mug with a horse's head on it, full to the brim with tea, Jenny said, "Don't worry about money, the bank's lending us some, so I can order some hay."

And I, brought up by cautious parents to be terrified of any debt, felt my heart sink again. "I expect we'll get some modelling soon and be able to pay it back. Would you like to drop in on Cynthia Abbott some time in her shop and see what she says?" suggested Jenny.

"Yes, and I'll draw some money out of my account and pay off the bank. I don't need the £400 still there," I replied quickly.

Jenny hugged me, saying that I was sweet, but that it was out of the question and that anyway Tommy's bill would be over £100, so that we were out of the wood. She said too that Alex was sending a cheque for Turpin's keep; and the payments for Faith and Hope would be coming in next week. "So no sleepless nights please Cathy," she finished.

I changed and searched my room for my Building Society book, without which I could not draw out any money, but without success. And all the while Vicky was running round and round me in circles wanting a walk, so I did that next, wandering round the fields, wishing that Tommy could stay. When I reached the yard again, Selina and her father had arrived with a horrible little trailer attached to an elderly Japanese car.

Jumping out of the car, Selina said straightaway, "I want my pony back. Where is he?" and her ghastly Dad added, "Selina's a real little horse-woman now."

"You told us not to ride Tommy and we haven't, so he may be a bit lively," I warned them, as Jenny appeared from the house. But Mr Reeves smiled a stupid smile and said, "Don't worry, Selina will handle it, won't you my darling?" And fair-haired, mean-faced little Selina twisted her face into a smile and answered, "Yes Dad, I can handle it."

"I'm warning you," Jenny said, "I would get an older child to ride Tommy first, I really would."

"No one's riding Tommy but me. He's mine," replied Selina, "And I'm not having him spoilt by anyone else."

Tommy whinnied when he saw me and trotted across the field and he really did look lovely. Then Selina snatched his headcollar from me saying, "Give it to me. I can catch my own pony." But of course she couldn't. Tommy veered away from her and put his head in the air. I slipped the headcollar over his small Welsh ears and buckled it, while her father said, "Selina's a little out of practice, but it will come back, won't it darling?" But I knew it wouldn't, because riding and putting on headcollars are like learning to bike or swim - you never forget how to do it.

Handing Selina Tommy's rope, I said, "I hope you've got a proper stable for him this time with lots of bedding, and company. Ponies hate living alone. I mean would you like it? No friends ever, no Mum and Dad, just you by yourself, all the time?"

"I'm not talking to you, because it's none of your business," replied Selina.

It took two hours to get Tommy into that minute trailer. He kept going up the ramp and then looking round with an expression in his eyes which said, 'I don't want to leave here', so plainly that my eyes were constantly full of tears. We tried a lunge rein now behind his quarters and moved one hoof at a time. We tried oats and carrots and pony cubes. Then quite suddenly he gave in. I think Jenny was crying as we threw up the ramp and bolted it.

Selina's father delved into one of the pockets of the enormous grey anorak he was wearing and fished out a handful of crumpled notes. "There's £100 there. Go on, count them," he said handing them to Jenny.

I ran into the house because now I couldn't stop crying and, as I ran, I could hear him saying, in his awful, self-satisfied voice, "I always pay my debts on time." I threw myself on my bed and howled while Vicky tried desperately to lick away my tears.

A moment later, opening my room door, Jenny said, "Don't cry. We've done our best and no one can do more than that."

"But he didn't want to go. It was on his face. He was so happy with us. And you know he'll have an awful time with them, and he's so sweet," I wailed.

Later I sat with Jenny in her untidy kitchen drinking cider and eating a meal I did not taste, and she said, "Well, the £100 will help us feed the others."

"And Torchy will need a lot," I added stifling unshed tears. "Do you think anyone will want him?"

"Yes of course. But how such a famous horse can end up as he has, makes me ashamed to be British," Jenny answered.

When things are bad, take one day at a time, that's what Mum says, and that's what I tried to do now. I wanted to buy myself some new boots, Vicky had chewed mine, but my Building Society book was still missing. Jenny didn't seem to think it mattered. "Stop worrying, it will turn up," she kept saying, but the only person who turned up was red-haired Mark demanding a coffee percolator which he had lent Jenny. Fortunately she was out. I gave it to him without a word and when he asked where she was, I said that I had no idea. Bill turned up too during that gloomy week and patched up some fencing and replaced a loose tile on Jenny's roof. Then on the Wednesday evening the telephone rang. Once I had liked the telephone to ring but lately I had begun to dread it.

"Cathy, it's Les. I'm afraid we're bringing Turpin back. He's chucked off our new working pupil and she's in hospital. We're setting off now," he said.

"But..." I began.

"No buts. He's a menace," replied Les slamming down the receiver. Half an hour later we unloaded Turpin. He was soaked in sweat and his eyes were wild again. Les was on his own. "You've wasted our time and put our new working pupil in hospital," Les was seething with fury.

"I told you to try him first. I rode him and he was edgy, but he didn't throw me off," I said.

"He's mad, totally mad. And the sooner he's put down the better." Les's face was scarlet with rage. "He's a nut case," he said throwing up the ramp on his trailer. "And I won't be taking any more horses from you. No way."

"Fine," I replied. "And we won't be sending you any either."

Turpin hurried into his box and stood at the back, resting his haunches against the wall. "Perhaps we should ring Alex," I suggested.

"Have you got her number?" asked Jenny, who had just appeared and looked thunderstruck.

I shook my head and said, "He looks so miserable. What have they done to him?"

"We won't have him put down, not yet anyway," said Jenny.

"I think we need a vet," I suggested.

"That's out of the question. We can't afford one. We owe the local practice too much money already.

They won't come any more unless it's an emergency, and this isn't one," replied Jenny.

"I'll pay the bill."

"You can't, you've lost your Building Society book. Remember?"

"Stop paying me £10 a week for helping then. I don't want it any more, not ever, okay?" I shouted.

I didn't walk Vicky across the fields that evening. I was missing Tommy too much. I took her to the end of the drive and back and I thought, when I'm an adult I'm going to study the minds of horses. I'm going to be a great expert, the greatest, because no one ever looks into their mental state, not properly anyway. And Turpin is too young to die.

When I returned from my short walk Alice was looking at Turpin. "I was bored. I cut across the fields. So Turpin's back," she said.

"Les and Suzie think he should be put down," I replied. "But we won't do it, not yet anyway. He threw their working pupil off and she's in hospital. I don't think Turpin's bad really. I think he's just a bit mad." Then I told Alice about Turpin escaping from the garden, where he had been left by Tracey, and being found upside down in a pub car park. Some people don't listen to what you say; they just want to hear their own voices, but Alice wasn't like that. She listened avidly and when I stopped talking she said, "We need to be detectives Cathy."

And then of course I thought, she's crazy too. We went into Turpin's box together. Alice asked me what he had been like when I rode him. When I had finished telling her, she said, "It all fits together like a jigsaw. And just look at him now, he's in pain, poor fellow, look at his eyes, Cathy. Look at the way he's standing."

"You mean it's not sweet itch this time," I said. "It's something else?"

"Yes, and I think I know what it is," replied Alice, running a hand down Turpin's spine. "It's his back."

"We need a vet then." As I spoke, I felt hope come back. Perhaps he will be all right after all, I thought.

"No, not exactly a vet; but a back man," said Alice, confidently smiling.

"And X-rays?" I asked.

"Perhaps."

I had never realised before how comforting it was to be with Alice. She was always the same and that was probably why the horses loved her.

"You know we haven't any money to pay a vet," I said next.

"The same old story. But I'm going to get someone I know; he may be retired by now, but if he can come, our problems with Turpin may be over," said Alice going out of the loose box and shutting the loose box door after her. "And I will pay for all his treatment."

"But..." I began and I was about to add, "But you're too poor to pay our bills," when she stalled me by saying, "And I can afford to pay, Cathy. I'm not a pauper. Come on, let's go in and tell Jenny."

The next day the back man came; nearly bald, small and quick, he did not waste time; he felt Turpin's back, pulled his legs this way and that, laughed and called Turpin, 'his old friend.' "My name is Dominic Childer." He smiled at Jenny and said, "I learnt my trade from gypsies and they don't have X-ray machines. I do it all by feel; it's cheaper. Poor old chap, his back *is* out of line, but never mind, just rest him for a few days and I'll come back next week and work on him a bit more," he said, straightening up and smiling at us.

"Is that all? Is he going to be all right now?" I asked.

"Sure. Alice told me he was found upside down in a car park; that could have started the problem, and being on a tether hardly helped, particularly if the chain was heavy. People don't think, that's the problem, one act of defiance and they shoot the horse, but of course it isn't defiance, it's because of excruciating pain; that's why he was throwing his head about when you were riding him, Cathy."

I wondered then how many horses were destroyed because of back trouble every year. 'What a waste,' I thought. "I was afraid he might be mad. Have a tumour or something," I said.

"Ah well, the symptoms are quite different. You tend to get fits with a tumour," replied Dominic Childer laughing. "And I won't be charging for my visit, you are doing a good job here. I'll ring you tomorrow to hear how the poor chap is."

When he had gone we all felt much better.

"What a lovely man," Jenny said.

"What a wonderful vet," I added.

"And all thanks to you Alice, you are a genius. I never considered his back causing the problem," said Jenny. "You do live and learn, don't you?"

"Are you going to ring up Les and tell him?" I asked.

"Not now, not yet."

Alice stayed to supper that night and opening a bottle of red wine, we celebrated Turpin's recovery.

The next few days were lovely, late summer days. Turpin was really better already. It was like a miracle.

Jenny rang the Sea Top Riding School and spoke to Suzie, who apologised profusely for Les's behaviour. She explained that their rates had leapt up because the Council had assessed the covered school as factory space, and that for two days they had been in despair and so Turpin bucking off their pupil had been the straw that broke the camel's back. Jenny, having given up her riding school for the same reason, said she understood and was sorry. Suzie then explained that they were now all right, since Riding for the Disabled were coming two mornings a week, and that a private school had booked in for Wednesday afternoons in term time. Then she had apologised all over again.

It was still just light enough to ride in the evenings after school and Josh and I discovered a new bridle way which went for miles. Mark was quiet for the moment; but Bill was still upset over the fate of Newhouse Farm. In the evening he sat on his stool in the kitchen, talking about it. "It's going on the market. Dave is moving out. They're finding him a Council house," he told us.

"What about the dogs?" I asked.

"They'll be put down; they're too savage for private homes," he said.

I imagined Newhouse Farm cleaned up; the ivy torn from the walls of the house, the rats destroyed;

the chicken houses swept away. Dave must have been just one of those people who start with good intentions; he must have meant to breed a show herd of Shetland ponies, but never thought the idea through, never considered the work, the bills, the bad summers and cold winters.

"He couldn't afford the vet bills, or the feed. He was all right until his brother was killed in a road accident. He never got over it," Bill continued.

The bills, I thought. And fate. Fate must have had a hand in it too and I was right, for the next thing Bill said was, "They had an epidemic. It killed his herd. He couldn't afford a vet; he hadn't the money."

And now I saw the same thing happening to us. If only we could win the lottery, if only we were better at raising money, if only we could just stop worrying, life would be heaven. But we won't win the lottery, I thought. We'll just have to go on struggling and then one day we will have an epidemic. Jenny had gone quiet. When Bill stopped talking, she asked, "What was the epidemic, Bill? I think we should know, don't you?"

"I don't want to upset you. I may have got it wrong, but Dave said it was a disease called strangles. It's a killer, he said, unless you get it in time," replied Bill.

Jenny had turned pale, while I thought, if we can't afford a vet, we can't afford an epidemic. Then I remembered the money I had in my Building Society book and felt better.

"Why didn't you tell us before? Straightaway? Now we had better keep the Shetlands in complete isolation. They must have their own grooming tools and their own buckets and if they have caught it and have runny noses we must act immediately," Jenny said in a hard hostile voice.

"We've done all that, haven't we, Cathy?" asked Josh who had just come in. "We've been ultra careful because of the lice, which have all gone now thank God, and because of the way they looked when they came here."

"And they are eating all right," I said.

"We'll take their temperatures every day and watch their eyes for inflammation and their throats for swellings. At the first sign of anything suspicious we'll call a vet," said Jenny.

"I'll pay as soon as I can find my Building Society book," I cried.

"We'll put a bucket of disinfectant outside their box and a tray full of disinfectant for your boots, and now I think I had better ring Lisa and tell her the bad news," announced Jenny standing up.

"It may not happen," said Josh, looking at me. "We haven't watered them at a communal water trough or anything like that and they can't see over their box door."

"But we've taken Beechnut for walks," I said, "And hung her headcollar in the tack room."

"But she hasn't got strangles, so she can't be infectious and the little mare hasn't even had a runny nose, so I think we will be all right," replied Josh sensibly.

"I'll ring Lisa," Jenny said again, hurrying to the telephone.

We waited in silence until Jenny put down the

telephone receiver. "It's all right, Beechnut had strangles years ago. I spoke to Lisa's Mum. She says that older horses often don't catch it, so we may be all right, but we must be really careful. They haven't been turned out so the paddocks are okay. But we mustn't take any chances, all right?"

We nodded; for a moment things seemed to be getting better. Turpin's back had recovered; Fantasy was putting on weight at last. The Welsh cobs, Hope and Faith, had been seen cantering around their paddock bucking.

Another day passed and another. We had all looked up strangles in our veterinary books by this time and knew that the incubation of the disease varied from two to fourteen days and that it often starts among foals and I remembered the skeletons at Newhouse Farm and imagined the same happening at Horsehaven. Vicky was growing bigger all the time and I still could not find my Building Society book.

One day Gillian and Sarah appeared and Sarah asked me whether I could keep a secret and I replied that I wasn't sure; but she said she would tell it to me anyway because it was so wonderful she couldn't believe it was happening. We were in the tack room with the wonderful smell of saddle soap all around us. "We're moving," she said, suddenly starry eyed. "Not far, quite near here. Granny's coming to live with us in an annexe of our house. It's big and it's got stabling and four acres."

"But that's wonderful, absolutely brilliant!" I cried.

"And we are going to have ponies, one each. Gillian wants to have Turpin. Do you think she can?" Sarah gazed at me with such hope that I said," "Of course, why not? But we'll have to inspect the place first, you know the rules." And we were both laughing now. "And I want Goldie until I'm too big for him and then maybe I'll have Turpin and Gillian will get something bigger," Sarah told me.

"I'm so pleased," I said.

"Mummy isn't, she says that there's enough hay on the floor after we've been here, so what it will be like when we have our own stables?" Sarah continued. "We're having a dog too, a rescued one, and bantams and I'm having a lovely bedroom looking out on the stables. I can't believe it's happening, but it is, I know it is, because Dad signed the contract yesterday. Do you think Turpin will be happy with us?" she went on.

"Very, but we'll have to talk to Alex first," I said.

Everything seemed fine that evening. Jenny had found herself an accountant, who was putting the accounts in order for the tax man. He was called Charles and was tall with dark hair and wonderful manners. He opened doors for us and said things like "Excuse me", and "Am I in the way?" and he thanked us ten times for every cup of coffee we gave him. Josh was to say later that Charles must have fancied Jenny from the start because it would have been much easier for him to take our accounts to his office and do them there. As for Jenny, she did seem happier, washing her hair every other day and rubbing a whole pot of hand cream into her worn hands. It turned out that Miles, who had been keeping the accounts for us, had blundered several times and they were now in a terrible state.

One evening I went to Cowford to see Cynthia Abbott who had previously hired me and some of the ponies for modelling her winter clothes for teenagers. There was a notice across her window which read CLOSING DOWN SALE. *Everything must go.* So it was with sinking heart, I pushed open her shop door and called, "Hi, anyone at home?"

"Oh it's you. Come in. Coffee?" I had forgotten how pretty Cynthia was with dark hair and expressive brown eyes.

"I haven't got time now ,thanks all the same. But why are you closing down?" I asked. "What's happened?"

"I can't afford the Council rates. A charity shop is buying me out; they don't have to pay the same rates as the rest of us. I just can't afford thousands of pounds every year. But don't worry Cathy," she continued, putting an arm around me. "I'm going into Mail Order, world wide, so I shall need you even more in the future. I'm just stuck until everything's sold and then I'll be expanding into Europe, Asia and the US."

"Brilliant. We'll be ready for you any time and though Rosa's gone, we've got an enormous and famous showjumper called Night Time Torchlight, Torchy for short."

"The Company, Night Time, was his sponsor, wasn't it?" asked Cynthia.

"Yes, but years ago. He's worn out now," I replied.

"He's got splints on both his front legs and windgalled fetlocks."

"And Night Time make everything for the night, is that right?" Cynthia asked.

"Yeah, they did but I think they went broke last year," I replied, looking around the half empty shop.

I said goodbye, ran home to Horsehaven and, bursting into the kitchen, cried, "Cynthia still wants us. She's going into Mail Order and she wants us as soon as her shop has closed down. So we will be world wide too."

Jenny was drinking coffee - she drinks far too much. "Turpin's got a temperature," she said. "He's coughing and there's a disgusting discharge coming from out of his nose. In other words he's got strangles."

I thought then of Gillian wanting him so much, I thought, 'strangles can kill, and what about Alex, will she ever forgive us?' I imagined the disease spreading throughout the stables. And now I couldn't get the rain-washed skeletons at Newhouse Farm out of my mind.

"Alice has gone home to call her vet out, not Dominic, another one. She says he'll come and that if you've got a title, everyone thinks you are solvent, whatever, which is obviously plain stupid," said Jenny and began to cry.

# CHAPTER SIX

## "HE'S VERY SICK"

The vet injected antibiotics into Turpin and told us everything we knew already from reading our veterinary books. He told Alice that he would return next day. Jenny had rung Alex by this time who, it seemed, was not upset and had said simply, "Well, either he gets better or he doesn't." Jenny had told her about his back too. "Oh well this is the third thing then, isn't it - first the sweet itch, then the back and now this? I think it's fate. I think we must leave it to fate, don't you?" Alex had asked.

Jenny told us all this and added, "I think she's very hard. I think her mother was a fool keeping Turpin for her; after all, she wouldn't have filled his loose box with her things, if she'd loved him."

"I think she's moved on. He was like a toy, which she grew out of. Of course it's easier with teddy bears; you can drop them off at OXFAM and feel good afterwards," I said.

Turpin stood at the back of his box and soon he wouldn't eat anything. The next day he was worse, the day after worse still. I had never seen a horse look so ill before. He didn't lie down at all and he would only take tiny sips of water, when we held a bucket under his nose.

The vet came again. He wore a white coat and plastic gloves now.

"He's very sick," he told us, sticking a needle into his neck. "You must be prepared for the worst. We may have to put him down. We don't want him to suffer do we?"

Gillian and Sarah knew how ill he was now. They stood peering over his box door, with tears streaming down their faces. I still couldn't forget Newhouse Farm. So many of the ponies there must have died one after another without a drop of medicine. Alice poulticed Turpin's gullet with a paste called Kaolin which she heated up in an old saucepan in the kitchen. All Turpin's head appeared swollen now. "If we can get the abscess to burst, he may get better quite quickly," Alice said, indomitable as ever. She was with us nearly all the time now. Gradually Turpin's temperature went up and up. His stomach became run up like a greyhound's. His haunches were gaunt and his eyes full of suffering.

On the third day, I said to Alice, "Perhaps it would be kinder to have him put down, because he's not going to get better is he? And he's in pain all the time. Just look at his eyes."

"Don't be ridiculous. Would you want to be put down if you were very ill with, say, meningitis, Cathy?" Alice asked, looking shocked.

I shook my head. Like everyone else who entered Turpin's box she wore surgical gloves and Wellington boots. Mrs Sykes had wanted to remove Regent as soon as she knew about Turpin, but Jenny had said that no other stable would have him and the vet backed her up, saying that any movement of any horse anywhere was out of the question. He was not a particularly nice vet. He was, as Josh said, 'stiff and formal and not very friendly'.

"Turpin should be put on a drip, if he is to be saved," insisted Josh. But the vet said that he would have to be moved elsewhere for that and that he was too infectious to be moved anywhere. He added that he had only ever seen one other horse with strangles and that had proved fatal.

I went to school and cried. I was sent to see the headmaster, who asked me whether I had trouble at home, and I said, "Only a pony dying." He said that I must not let it get in the way of my work, and that we all had to ride out storms in our lives. Then he said, could he do anything to help? I shook my head. I felt a fool for crying. I wanted to be strong and cool-headed. I wished I was someone else - preferably a tall blonde with blue eyes, who went through life smiling, whatever the odds; the sort of woman you see on Bond films. But I wasn't and I knew I would never change. After school I returned to Horsehaven and nothing there seemed to change either.

"He's just the same, Cathy," Jenny told me. "Alice says we're reaching crisis point. She's been poulticing his abscess again and it's getting more and more solid. She thinks it should be lanced. He won't even take a sip of water any more and you should see the stuff coming out of his poor nose."

The other horses were still all right, even the foals. But we could not use the long field any more, because Turpin had been in it, so the ground was now infected.

76

Gillian and Sarah did not appear during that weekend. Their mother rang to say that they were too distraught and that they were all flying to Disneyland in Paris to take their minds off Turpin. Josh and I soldiered on, while Charles appeared and sat in the kitchen talking to Jenny. And Vicky carried away brushes and ropes and buried them in the muck heap.

Alice only looked after Turpin now. We called her his nurse. Torchy grew increasingly impatient with us and kept staring into the distance, as though he thought he should be going somewhere and when we led him past the trailer, he always stopped and seemed to be saying, 'let's go.' After so much show jumping his legs were scarred. His Roman nose gave him an air of disdain. He was not a cuddly horse.

Mrs Sykes kept Regent stabled all the time now. She would not ride in the covered school because I had ridden Turpin there. She wrote Regent's name on a water bucket and a feed bin and tied a label to a hay net on which was written, FOR REGENT ONLY. We were terrified that Turpin might have infected the Sea Top Riding School with strangles, while he was there, yet none of us dared warn them of the possibility. Alice kept saying that Turpin was not infectious while he was incubating the disease, but Alice wasn't a vet and none of us dared asked the unfriendly vet, who was so sniffy about the Kaolin poultices Alice applied and held out such little hope, that we dreaded his occasional visits.

The sun shone, which made everything seem worse. Gillian and Sarah returned from Paris and telephoned: "Is he all right? Is he better?" shrieked Sarah and we all knew who 'he' was. "Has his lump burst?" asked Gillian.

I had answered the telephone and I said, "He's just the same, only thinner."

"It was awful being away, we kept thinking about him all the time and a French man wanted to know why we were crying," Gillian said.

"While there's life, there's hope," I said quoting Alice.

"The French man said that a pony wasn't worth a young girl's tears," continued Gillian, as though I had not spoken.

"Oh yuk, how absolutely yuk of him. He had probably just eaten horse for lunch and enjoyed it," I replied. "And whenever he looks at an animal, he thinks about eating it. 'Shall I grill it or bake it? What do you think wife? Or cover it with sauce?' he says." Though it wasn't a giggling matter, we all giggled.

"Mum's coming to fetch you. She wants to show you our new place," Gillian said next. "Oh I do hope we can have Turpin."

"If he recovers, he'll take at least two months to get over his strangles," I replied.

"We can wait," replied Gillian. "See you in half an hour."

Their place was indescribably lovely with a huge oak tree on a sun dappled lawn, under which grey squirrels were gathering nuts. There was a small orchard, a field of nearly five acres and a stable with two stalls, which would be converted later into loose boxes, plus a harness room with the old fittings still there; and a building beneath a loft, which they called the gig house. The house was ancient too and full of space, and the atmosphere was one of peace. The annexe was on one side with a conservatory, which led on to a second smaller lawn. As I looked at it all, I was filled with the most terrible envy; at the same time I knew that Turpin would be happy there. Josh, who was with us, said that it was a place left in a time warp. Gillian and Sarah's mother bemoaned the ancient high ceilinged kitchen where we drank coffee, saying that it would be freezing cold in winter.

When we returned to Horsehaven, we found Alice boiling a knife in a saucepan on the kitchen stove. "I'm going to lance Turpin's abscess. It's our only hope," she said.

I thought that Alice looked like a witch, watching the boiling saucepan, wearing a headscarf, an old cardigan over a jersey and grey trousers. I did not notice how tired she was, nor saw how her hand shook, as she lifted out the knife with a pair of tongs. My head was still full of envy, for I too wanted a large house with paddocks and stabling. I too wanted my own pony. It was what I had always wanted.

"I'll hold his head," offered Jenny, standing up.

They went out together. Vicky sat on my knee and licked my face and I imagined Mum saying, "Don't let her do that, it isn't hygienic." Then Josh and I went outside to watch Alice at work.

"She should have been a vet," I said.

"She wanted to, but the war got in the way," replied Josh.

"Is she that old then?"

"I'm afraid so," replied Josh.

"She's not like a titled person," I suggested next, not for the first time.

"A title doesn't mean anything," replied Josh. "The most awful wimps and creeps have titles."

We leant on the loose box door. Turpin didn't resist the knife. As we watched, I saw that he had suddenly grown old. I thought of Alex, who had not bothered to visit him. I thought that if Dad could see us, he would say we should be nursing people not horses.

Turpin didn't move as Alice lanced his abscess. She had a bowl of warm antiseptic with her and mounds of lint. Suddenly pus was streaming down her arms thick as clotted cream. Did Turpin's eyes lighten a little then or did I imagine it?

"Well done, you're a genius Alice," Jenny said.

"At least he's easier now," she replied. "And perhaps he'll eat tomorrow and then we can give him his medicine. But of course he's still critical. Do you mind if I go inside now? I feel so tired all of a sudden. I need to sit down for a little while."

That evening we made Turpin a bran mash. He was lying down by the time we gave it to him, not stretched out like a horse in pain but facing the door with his ears pricked and his hoofs folded neatly underneath him. Alice had warned us that the poison might have got into his blood stream. "He's not recovered yet," she had said. So we mixed antibiotics in his mash and grated apple and carrot and a few grains of garlic. We put it under his nose and he ate a little slowly and painfully. We fetched him water with glucose in it and he drank a few mouthfuls then sighed a long sigh.

"He would be dying if it wasn't for Alice," I said.

"Or dead, because we couldn't afford the vet bills," replied Josh.

"And she isn't rich," I added.

"She told me she had nothing else to spend her pension on," answered Josh. "She hasn't any relations and her husband died twenty years ago."

The next day we named the two foals. The two foals were dark brown, the mare black. We named the mare Morag which is a Scottish name, and the largest foal Kelpie which Josh said was the name of a Scottish water sprite - sometimes I think Josh is a walking encyclopaedia - and the other one Rocky.

Turpin was a little better already. We did not need a vet or even Alice to tell us that. The terrible gloom, which had hung over the yard for days now, lifted. The sun shone. Kelpie and Rocky appeared to be growing before our eyes and there was no sign of any other of our charges developing strangles. Jenny, having borrowed money from the bank, had loads of hay delivered. Gillian and Sarah talked unceasingly about their house.

Mum rang to say that Dad had been put in charge of the whole caravan site and that they were moving into a house. "You must come and see us soon; there's loads of room," Mum said. "And a lovely garden and your Dad's got two men working under him now."

And half of me wanted to go and half of me wanted

to stay, as September became October and the evenings grew darker. One day, when I returned from school, I found Turpin turned out in the long field. He was still pathetically thin, but he looked happy and was covered with mud, having rolled.

"We're so lucky," said Jenny joining me, "Because strangles could have spread through the stables like wildfire, and then we would have been finished and just a little longer, and we will be in the clear."

"Did he catch it from Morag?" I asked.

"I guess so; she had a bit of a runny nose when she came. I just didn't think fast enough. We should have started wearing plastic gloves and taken precautions straightaway."

Bill had not been to see us for some time now. Maybe he was helping his old comrade Dave to move, or maybe he had grown tired of us, Jenny said.

Mrs Sykes had given in her notice. As far as Regent was concerned he was being moved as soon as possible to some smarter stables which specialised in dressage facilities.

"I've had enough of your lame ducks," she told Josh. "And as for strangles, that was a disaster waiting to happen, wasn't it?"

"We've always done our best and nobody can do more than that Mrs S," replied Josh philosophically.

"But sometimes, best isn't good enough," replied Mrs Sykes.

She had always paid a good fee and we would miss that, but on the other hand as a charity we probably should not have been taking liveries at all. Charles had already pointed that out to Jenny once and Charles knew about the law and taxes and what was acceptable in life and what wasn't. Recently I had started to feel in the way, when he was in Jenny's house, for one thing he was really tall and seemed to fill up the whole kitchen. But he was reliable and dependable and Jenny was beginning to lean on him more and more, and as Josh was to say one day, at least he was the opposite of Jenny's Mark in every possible way. He understood horses too, having once been what he called, 'a pony club boy.'

So October became November and the trees along the drive to Horsehaven lost their leaves, and rain fell for days on end.

I was doing better at school and perhaps best of all, neither Vince nor Sammy had been to visit us for several weeks.

Gillian and Sarah moved into their new house and a date was fixed for Turpin to go there. Lisa and her mother fetched Beechnut and the Shetlands were turned out into a far field with a hedge round it for the winter. The owners of Hope and Faith were fined £600 for cruelty and banned from keeping horses for ten years. Jenny said that it was not enough. Alice said that they should have been given a taste of prison.

Soon after that, Hope and Faith were found new homes. I did not see them go. I was at school that day. But Jenny said that they were to be used for breeding and since they had not been rescued by us we had no say in the matter.

Charles, who was often at Horsehaven now, told me to stop worrying and to try to enjoy life more. I was beginning to like him, for he was always the same; nothing seemed to upset him. Josh liked him too and as for Gillian and Sarah, they followed him everywhere and wouldn't have a word said against him.

# CHAPTER SEVEN

## TOMMY RETURNS

Regent left, bandaged and rugged in an enormous horsebox. Josh started to ride Torchy, who wasn't traffic proof, and shied a lot. Turpin and Goldie left to live with Sarah and Gillian. Prince neighed for hours afterwards. Fog descended, freezing and obliterating. I went to see Mum and Dad in their new house, which was immaculate with new furniture and a fitted kitchen. They showed me my bedroom. There was a china label on the door, saying, *Catherine*. Looking at it, I felt a right heel.

"Well! What do you think?" Mum asked.

"Brilliant, fantastic," I replied. "But what about Vicky, isn't the house a bit clean for a puppy?" and I recalled Jenny's house with mud on the door mat and bits of hay on the carpets.

"I don't mind. I don't like it so tidy. I want it to look homely," replied Mum.

Feeling guilty again, I hugged her. "When I'm older I'll live here with you. It's so brilliant to know I've got a room. If Jenny marries Charles, I will come straightaway." (It was the first time it had occurred to me that Jenny might marry Charles.)

"How are you managing, money wise?" Mum wanted to know next. "Are you fund-raising? A jumble sale? Bingo?"

I shook my head and at the same time realised

that we were now not making any money, since all our liveries had gone.

When I returned to Horsehaven, Josh was sweeping the yard. "Vince has been here looking for you. Is there something going on between you?" he asked laughing.

"No way," I said. "You know that, Josh. You know I hate him."

"He doesn't seem to think so, and another thing, Jenny's been sent a sale catalogue and Tommy's in it. He's described as a liver chestnut Welsh Section pony. I don't know which section, it doesn't say. Jenny rang Mr Reeves straightaway to ask about him and got Selina instead, and she said that Tommy had hurt her real bad and she had had stitches in her leg."

"Goodie," I said spitefully. And then, "Oh don't look at me like that Josh, you know how awful she is and I don't really mean it."

"Jenny says she's buying Tommy back," Josh said.

"Where's the money coming from?"

"I don't know. I didn't ask."

"Well there isn't any, is there?" I said and then, remembering Mum's remarks, "And when are we going to hold something?"

"I'm doing photo Christmas cards. We can sell them into shops and pubs, and stand at street corners," Josh said. "We'll give some to Sammy to sell, and to Vince."

"You know he would just pocket the money and spend it on lager or drugs," I replied.

"Miles is doing the inside on his computer. Mum's getting boxes, so we can sell them as assorted. It was Sammy's idea," Josh told me.

I didn't want to talk about Sammy. I wished she didn't exist. Turpin had gone. Torchy made it obvious that he preferred Josh to me. The Welsh cobs had gone. One day Trooper would go too and then I would be heartbroken.

"There's a show quite near in a covered school. Jenny says that we can take Trooper and Torchy if we like. She thinks it's time they were re-homed," said Josh confirming my worst fears. "So I was thinking that we could jump Trooper and Torchy tomorrow," continued Josh and then of course I felt torn apart because I had never competed in a horse show before; at the same time I did not want Trooper to win prizes or be admired because then he would find a home and be lost to me forever.

"I've been on my own all afternoon. It's been brilliant, not even Alice around, and Jenny and Charles have gone to the cinema together," continued Josh.

"When did Vince come?" I asked.

"So you are interested in him then?" laughed Josh. "He came at twelve o'clock if you want to know."

I threw an empty bucket at Josh, but he only laughed in a stupid, superior way, which made my blood boil.

The next day we schooled Torchy and Trooper in the covered school. Torchy jumped at least a metre over all our 100cm fences. Trooper knocked everything down. I think that, from that day, Josh fell in love with Torchy. I think he saw himself competing at Wembley on him in the years ahead.

I think he forgot that Torchy was an old horse, who had had his day. He took him on, became responsible for him and Torchy responded, whinnying whenever he saw him, his old face with the deep sockets above his eyes lighting up. It was too dark to ride out after school now, but most evenings we rode for half an hour or more in the covered school. Trooper began to go better. I schooled him over poles on the ground building up his confidence, while Josh seemed to be jumping ever higher fences. By this time I believe Jenny was falling in love with Charles, because she didn't seem to notice what was going on and so Josh and I had the yard to ourselves most of the time.

Winter was late coming that year; the grass was still growing in November. Gillian rang to say that they had started riding Turpin very gently and that he was going like a dream, and that Goldie could now do a turn on the haunches and was jumping half a metre. November became December and Josh and I spent a whole evening in my room boxing up the Christmas cards he and Miles had made between them. There was one with Trooper on the front and another of Torchy looking out over his loose box door; there were two of Squid and Fidget looking cuddly in their long winter coats and three of Rocky and Kelpie taken long distance so you could not see how thin they were. Printed on the back of each card was: IN AID OF HORSEHAVEN HORSE AND PONY SANCTUARY. There were eight cards in a box priced at £2.50 and I took three boxes for Mum to sell. I remember feeling incredibly happy at that time. Trooper seemed almost

mine and I was going to my first ever show. Josh
and I were together again. Vicky was growing into
a responsible little dog, who barked at strangers
and would come when called, retrieve a ball and
sit when told.

Alice did not come early in the morning any more;
so I had the yard to myself. Of course I should
have been worried by Alice's absence but my life
seemed brimful of things to do. Besides, I felt it
was Jenny's job to worry about her, but as she was
falling in love with Charles, which was plain for
all to see, she had no time to worry about anything.

One day I returned from school to find Tommy in
his old loose box again. He called to me like an old
friend.

"Now we haven't got Gillian and Sarah any more,
I'm handing him over to you to school," announced
Jenny coming out of the house. "You're light
enough, just walk him at first in the school. Don't
ride out on him alone. I've bought his tack too, it's
very stiff, and the bridle's not properly adjusted.
It looks as though dear little Selina was riding
with the bit literally between his teeth."

"Was he expensive?" I asked wondering where
the money had come from.

"A few hundred. By the way, I've had an offer for
the wood and it's enough money to solve all our
problems for quite some time," said Jenny who can
never keep a secret.

"The wood, our wood? I mean your wood, but it's
so lovely," I cried. "Is someone going to build houses
on it?"

"No just manage it properly, cut down the present trees for timber and replant. Apparently beech is worth quite a lot," replied Jenny in a matter of fact voice.

I looked at her wondering whether Charles had had anything to do with it.

"We don't use it for anything. I mean it's no good for horses is it?" Jenny smiled at me.

"But the trees are hundreds of years old, and what about the bluebells? And you know nobody will replant it with beeches, because they take too long to grow. Oh Jenny you can't," I cried.

"I may have to. I don't want to, but if we're to survive it may be my only option."

"But we've got so few horses now, it's ridiculous," I replied. "And once I start modelling again, and we've sold all the Christmas cards we will have loads of money." I was shouting now. "Can't you see we're going to be all right? Just give us time."

"There's no need to shout. I'm not deaf and I'm sick of living hand to mouth, and everything's going up - the telephone, the electricity, the rates, everything," replied Jenny glaring at me. She was talking as my parents used to talk, when Dad had no job and we couldn't pay the mortgage.

"What does Charles say?" I asked next.

"It's nothing to do with him. If I make a decision it will be mine and mine alone," replied Jenny tersely.

If I had been older, I would have bought myself a lottery ticket and hoped to win a million. But I was too young. I told Josh what Jenny had said.

"Damn. I was planning to build a cross country

90

course for Torchy in the wood. Still, if trees are felled we can use them as jumps can't we?" he asked.

"But it won't be our wood any more. Can't you understand? She's selling it Josh, for ever and ever."

But Josh did not want to understand; all he could talk about was Torchy. I took Vicky for a walk in the wood and the huge, bare trunked trees made me think of a cathedral; they were so noble and still and stately. I thought of them lying felled like fallen giants, years of growth struck down in minutes by the screeching of a chain saw. I thought of the bluebells trampled to nothing in the spring by greedy machines dragging out the slain trees. The wood would be like a battlefield, after a battle which we had lost. I wept as I turned back to the stables and I thought if Jenny can sell the wood so lightly, what will she sell next?

At supper that night, I said, "If you sell the wood I'll go, Jenny, you know that, don't you? I don't want to see the trees falling, because they're like friends to me and cutting them down is murder in my eyes."

But Jenny insisted that she had not come to a decision yet; the offer was simply on the table. She said, not for the first time, "Don't jump your fences before you come to them;" and then, that I took life far too seriously. I pointed out that we now had only eight horses and three of them were Shetlands so hardly counted and she said, "You've forgotten Tommy."

"But we've got a barn full of hay already," I cried,

91

unrepentant.

"Thanks to a loan," she said.

"I've been so happy recently and now you are spoiling everything," I cried. "It's been lovely seeing Turpin get well and the foals and Morag; and Torchy is jumping like a dream and Trooper is going better every day. Something will turn up, it always has before," I told Jenny taking my supper plate to the sink, pleased that for once Charles wasn't with us.

The next day I rode Tommy. I was far too large for him but he didn't seem to mind. I walked and trotted him round the covered school without any problems. Josh was watching. "I expect Selina hung on by her heels and was then surprised the poor pony took off. I wonder where she had her riding lessons," he said.

Later Sammy appeared to collect her Christmas cards. Even more beautiful than before, she hugged me like an old friend. "Oh it's great to see you again Cathy, it really is," she cried.

And I, who had always seen her as a foe, was suddenly struck speechless.

"Has Vince been around lately?" she asked next.

"Sure," I said. "And he hasn't changed."

"You know he's crazy about you," continued Sammy. "He really is."

"He's wasting his time then because I can't stand the sight of him. Okay," I said.

"Poor Vince, he's always wasting his time," replied Sammy laughing. She knelt on the ground and talked to Vicky while I told her about the fate of the wood hanging in the balance, and how the

Sea Top Riding School was struggling to survive because of the enormous rates the Council was charging it, and about Gillian and Sarah's lovely house and about Charles and Jenny. She laughed and said that nothing had changed really, and she didn't believe it ever would. "Only the horses change, you go on just the same, Cathy, and I admire you for it," she said, and then I hated her again for being patronising.

Times were changing. Miles did not show up any more because Charles was now in charge of the accounts. Jenny insisted that Charles was putting Horsehaven on a proper financial footing, but that the outlook was bleak, because without the liveries she could no longer pay herself a wage, nor me my £10 a week.

"But you haven't paid me for ages and I don't mind," I cried. "I don't need the money because Mum lets me have my child allowance, and when I find my book I can draw some money out of the Building Society for Christmas presents. If I don't find it soon, I'll have to report it missing to the Building Society; that's what Mum says."

"Clever Mum," replied Jenny.

"And the Christmas cards will make a few hundred pounds," I said.

Jenny did not reply. I guessed that she was thinking,' a few hundred pounds, but that's chicken feed, it's thousands we need.'

Later that evening Vince called. I found him hanging about the yard as I went out after tea. "Here you are," he said. I made it for you, for this place really," he said, handing me an envelope.

Inside was £100.

"But how?" I cried, at the same time calling, "Come and look Jenny, Vince has given us some money."

Vince said that he had made it doing shopping for an old lady but that did not sound much like Vince. Jenny and I stared at the money. "It's very good of you, but I don't think we can take it, not unless you tell us exactly where it came from," Jenny said, looking Vince straight in the eye.

"I told you didn't I, just now? I've been shopping for an old lady."

"Then can we have her address please?" Jenny asked.

Vince shuffled his feet. "I don't know it. I can't remember it, can I?" he replied.

"Can you show us her house then?" suggested Jenny.

"Look, I took it from a pub, it was in a money box. I reckoned you needed it more. I took the box to the toilet and transferred the money to myself. It was in aid of something stupid, so I took it," he said. "There's nothing wrong with that, is there?"

"Right, get in the Land Rover, we're taking it back. I said get in, Vince," shouted Jenny furiously.

I watched them leave. For the first time I pitied Vince, but it did not mean I liked him any more. At that moment I wished that he and Sammy would simply disappear for ever. Then I wished that the sky would rain money and now suddenly I was missing Alice.

# CHAPTER EIGHT

## AN ACCIDENT

The Christmas holidays had begun when Alice re-surfaced, explaining that she had had a little bit of a stroke and that one arm didn't work quite as well as the other. And she laughed, while we felt horribly guilty, for not knowing; but far worse, for not bothering about her.

"It's great to have you back. I've missed you," I said.

Josh hugged her. Alice said that she missed Turpin. "I keep seeing his head over his old door, but then it isn't there," she said. "But there's good news, Gillian and Sarah have asked me over to tea. It's so sweet of them."

Josh gave her a box of Christmas cards to sell. "They are going like hot cakes," he said.

That afternoon Josh and I rode in the covered school. Alice had gone home by this time. Charles was closeted inside the house with Jenny discussing money - or so they said!

The Christmas Horse Show was now only a week away. Josh and I both entered for several events. Josh said that Torchy was going to make a great comeback there and that he was going in for the Open Jumping. I had only entered Trooper for a class called First Timers, which was for riders and horses which had never competed before. Torchy was in Take Your Own Line too. I did not attempt the course Josh had built in our covered school that afternoon; it looked enormous; but Torchy was game. He pricked his old ears and his eyes shone as Josh called, "I'm riding him in a circle. Please make the sound of a bell when I'm to start." So a minute later I yelled, "Ting a ling. Start, go, there's a time limit." Torchy pranced, his hocks under him now, ready to perform, as he must have done so many, many times before.

Then they were off, over a brush fence, over parallel bars, on to the gate. (These were the fences left over from the days when Jenny ran a riding school). Josh's face was a mixture of concentration and sheer happiness as they approached the wall.

"Brilliant," I yelled as Torchy cleared it with lots to spare.

Now came the double, then an oxer, then a triple. But after the oxer Torchy seemed to be falling apart, his rhythm went, his stride became uneven, he lengthened out and then he was going down on to his forehand.

"Stop," I shouted too late. "Pull up."

But the triple bars were upon them now, Torchy appeared to stumble; another minute and he was in the midst of them, then struggling to get up, while I leapt off Trooper and ran across the school, shouting, "Are you all right?" Torchy stood up with blood pouring from his nose as fast as water from a tap. Josh held his head for a moment before he said, "It's my arm. I think it may be broken. Torchy fell on it, but it wasn't his fault, it was my fault. I didn't keep him together."

"Stay still, don't move. Neither of you move. Okay? Stay where you are," I shouted before I slid open the school doors, shut them after me and ran to the house shouting, "Help, help, there's been an accident." And Vicky who had been in the yard ran with me, yapping wildly at my heels.

Charles and Jenny were kissing in the kitchen. "Josh has had a fall and Torchy has a nose bleed. I think we may need an ambulance."

"Don't worry, I'll deal with it." Charles moved swiftly and decisively towards the door.

"What about dialling 999?"

"Not yet, let's assess the situation first," suggested Charles, putting on Wellies as though we had all the time in the world.

"He thinks he's broken his arm," I continued. "They fell into the triple bars. Torchy just ran out of steam. It was terrible."

"I told Josh not to expect too much of him. I told him he was an old horse," cried Jenny, furiously. "How could he have been so idiotic? He should never have built a big course for him. I thought I told both of you that, but then you never listen, do you?" Suddenly Jenny was sounding like my Mum.

Charles knelt beside Josh, talking to him. He took off the scarf he was wearing and made it into a sling. "I did first aid when I was in the army. I think it's only badly bruised. Come on old chap, I'll take you into hospital in my car for an X ray. Can you stand up?" he asked.

Jenny started to apply pressure to Torchy's nose, who still looked bemused and shaken. Poor old horse, his body must have simply let him down and the worry of it was all over his face, plus a look of disgrace and fear too as though he expected a beating for not having done better. I put my arms around his neck, before calling to Josh, "Do you want me to go to hospital with you?" Josh shook his head. "Mum's there working. I'll be all right. You look after Torchy."

Jenny and I led Trooper and Torchy back to the stables. "I think we'll forget the Show. They're both too old to compete any more. I'm sorry. I had no idea you were jumping such big fences," Jenny said.

"I wasn't," I replied.

"I would still rather you didn't go. I'll give you back your entrance fees. It was wrong from the start. Torchy's simply too old. He's meant to be retired," Jenny said.

"I don't want my money back. I don't need it. All I need is my Building Society book," I wailed. And I felt guilty now even though it wasn't me who had expected an old horse like Torchy to jump such a big course.

Torchy's nose started bleeding again when we reached the stables. He blew it and huge clots of blood flew in all directions.

"If it doesn't stop soon, we'll have to call a vet," Jenny said holding a bucket to catch the blood. But which one, I wondered? Alice's, whom we disliked or the usual ones, who might not want to come because of their unpaid accounts.

"Charles is very efficient," I said.

"Yes he is," replied Jenny, looking pleased.

"What about Mark wanting his money back?" I

asked next.

"His mum has given it to him. She rang to say not to worry any more about it."

I remembered his mum - bossy, interfering, but underneath it all with a heart of gold apparently. I thought, you can't judge people, not until you're in trouble and then your friends come out of the woodwork to help. But at that moment we didn't seem to have many friends.

"I think we should worry about Alice. She's so poor," I said next.

"Yes, and she's not well either, that's the worst part of it," replied Jenny.

"It's not as though she can afford help. I was thinking that Josh and I might offer to help, do her shopping or something," I suggested vaguely. "But now I suppose there's only me."

"She's still driving her own car and she's very independent-minded," replied Jenny. I'm telling you this because of what happened later. I want you to know that I did think about Alice; that I'm not totally uncaring.

Torchy's nose stopped bleeding. "We'll leave him to be quiet for a bit," said Jenny taking off his headcollar and patting him. "Do you want a coffee?"

We went indoors together. "I don't know how we'll manage if Josh is laid up," said Jenny wearily, switching on the kettle. "We need more helpers."

"We need so much," I answered.

"None of your gloom and doom, Cathy, please. Charles is going to restructure everything. He has an excellent business head," replied Jenny. "He's picked up several points already which hadn't

99

occurred to me. We just need an inflow of money, that's the overwhelming problem."

"As always, and help," I added.

But the only new helper who turned up was Vince. "I heard Josh had gone to hospital so I thought I would lend a hand," he said gloating.

"Brilliant," I said. "Here's a wheelbarrow and everything else you need."

Vince was strong, willing, but as thick as a plank. Now that winter was upon us, more and more of our inmates were being stabled at night - Torchy, Trooper, Fantasy and Morag, Kelpie and Rocky too because they were still like toast racks.

Josh was soon back, his arm in a sling, grooming Torchy with one hand. He wouldn't be helped. Vince glowered. It wasn't a good atmosphere and Alice, who might have softened it, still had not appeared. Jenny, obviously in love with Charles, said cheerfully, "Don't worry. I expect she's gone to friends for Christmas."

Josh and I sent her a Christmas card with: *See you soon, love Josh and Cathy,* written inside.

Vince did not mention the money he had had to return. He did not even look guilty. Josh said that he had no conscience. I said that he wasn't quite normal. Vicky was afraid of him. I was certain that he must have kicked her sometime, when I wasn't looking, but this he denied saying, "Why should I kick her? A silly thing like that?"

It was not a happy time. We all felt on edge and I think we were all missing Sarah and Gillian. Soon Vince was doing an enormous amount of work. He was tireless and always hungry. None of us was sure where he actually lived and I think we were all uneasy in his company. I hated being alone with him. And all the time I was scared that he might hurt Vicky. Josh, with one arm resting, was afraid to stand up to him and Jenny was forever saying, "You are keeping an eye on Vince, aren't you? Don't let him near any money," as though we had a mass of money lying around, and had to watch him. Vince blamed 'them' for the bad weather, his lack of education, just about everything, but none of us were sure who 'they' were - the government? TV? The weather forecasters? The DHSS? It was a mystery.

I planned to go to my parents for Christmas. Jenny said that she would manage somehow and not to worry. Vince promised to help; Jenny refused the offer, scared that he would want to share her Christmas dinner or help himself to things when she was out. Besides the horses did not like him. As Josh said, "It is a devil of a dilemma."

Two days before Christmas Jenny gave us Alice's address and Josh, Vicky and I went to see her. It was a freezing afternoon and everything was tinselled silver with frost. Alice lived in nearby Treadmill, a small village with a church, a few cottages, a sad looking shop run by a lady in her nineties, a pub which was usually empty and a workshop where you could buy pine furniture.

Alice lived in Rose Cottage. We expected something tumbledown, but it was really pretty with little windows and a thatched roof. But there was no smoke coming out of its chimney, the garden was overgrown and the front door step green with moss.

"I expect she uses the back door, most people do," said Josh.

The back door was unlocked. We found Alice in a small low ceilinged room asleep in front of a one bar electric fire with a cat on her knee. Waking with a start, she cried, "Oh, what a surprise! Where did you spring from?"

"We wanted to see if you were all right," said Josh.

"What is all right?" asked Alice, jumping up. "Would you like a cup of something? My doctor said I was not to be out in the cold; but I'll be back at the stables as soon as the weather picks up. How are all the dear horses? Tell me everything."

It was a relief to see that Alice was all right. We sat drinking tea and eating chocolate biscuits; then she showed us photographs of her winning at the Olympic Horse Show, whipping in to hounds, talking to the Queen; riding in a dressage test in a top hat. "You see I really was quite good," she said, showing us more and more photographs from her past, in which the riding clothes were very different from nowadays. Even the horses looked different. Far more of them wore double bridles and the little ponies all seemed to have cruppers attached to their saddles.

There were ours and a few other Christmas cards on a table and a little Christmas tree in a pot. "I'm going to a friend nearby to celebrate," Alice said, patting Josh on his hand. "So don't you go worrying about me, I shall be all right."

"Touch wood," I said. And laughing, we all touched a nearby table.

Alice's cat was called Cezanne after the painter. She told us that her husband had been called Hugh, but that she had never really cared for him. "He was all right until we got married and then he changed," she said with a tinkling laugh.

It was getting dark outside now. It was time to go. "Give my love to everyone," Alice said. "And I'm so sorry about your arm Josh. I broke my pelvis once riding at the Badminton Horse Trials and it was agony. I was too old of course. I was past forty by then."

On our way out we collected Vicky from the kitchen, where she was eating the cat's dinner. Walking back to Horsehaven, Josh said, "I'm glad we went, aren't you?"

"Definitely." Everything was freezing, even our breath.

"I wish she wasn't alone," Josh said next.

"She must have been so rich once," I said at the same moment. "And quite famous. But now she's all alone with her cat," I said.

"But happy," suggested Josh, putting his good arm through mine.

Everything looked so pure that evening, austere and beautiful, or maybe I saw it that way because Josh's arm was through mine and we were on our own.

When we reached Horsehaven we found Vince helping Jenny. "Oh there you are!" he exclaimed, glowering at Josh. "I want to show you something, Cathy. Come into the tack room."

Josh let go of my arm. "Go on, he can't eat you Cathy," he said laughing.

"I've had it done for you. Look!" cried Vince a minute later pulling up the sleeves of his dirty grey jerkin. "Just look at that, Cathy. Do yer like it? What do you think?" Tattooed on Vince's thick hairy arm was a drawing depicting a horse's head with 'Cathy' written beneath it. "It's Trooper, or maybe Fantasy, except that the ears aren't right," Vince said.

With horror I thought of it there for ever - my name on Vince's arm!

"You see there's a little heart there. Come nearer and look," he said.

"I can see it. But you should never have had it done," I cried. "It's such a waste of money," I added edging towards the door.

"Nothing's a waste for you Cathy," Vince said. "I just wanted you to see that I won't forget you, not ever, not as long as I live."

I ran across the yard into my room and shut the door. I had been so glad that we had visited Alice, now Vince was ruining everything.

# CHAPTER NINE

## "WAS SHE VERY OLD?"

Our Christmas cards made £112. Alex sent me a Christmas card, so did Gillian and Sarah, Les, Suzie, Bill and Sammy. Vince gave me the biggest one I had ever seen. It had cost £8 and I couldn't help wondering where he had found the money for it. I gave everyone our own cards, for which I had paid. Mum and Dad bought me clothes for Christmas; the sort I would never wear: patterned leggings, thick tights, a flowered blouse and slippers which Vicky took and chewed to pieces over Christmas, which made Mum cry when I told her. Josh gave me a novel by Dick Francis. I gave him a collection of Horse Stories and Jenny riding gloves. The weather changed and it rained all Christmas Day. Mum drove me back to Horsehaven on Boxing Day. "Did you like your room Cath?" she asked on the way.

"Yes, it's brilliant," I answered automatically and Mum said accusingly, "You don't mean that do you?"

"Yes I do. I love it, but it's not me, because I haven't got my things in it yet," I replied.

Mum didn't stay long at Horsehaven. She hates it really, because she feels it's taken me from her, and I suppose she's right in a way.

Vince was in the kitchen, drinking coffee with

Jenny. He held his arms out to me as though he was my boyfriend.

I stepped back and cried, "Don't touch me. I don't belong to you or anyone else. I don't want to, not ever, so get that into your thick head, Vince, once and for all." Without meaning to, I was shouting.

Josh was there too. It was like any other morning, except that for me the very air felt fraught with danger now.

To change the subject, Jenny said, "Cathy, you haven't asked after the horses," while Josh asked, "Why don't you leave Cathy alone, Vince? You can't make anyone love you. It's a fact of life and no amount of tattoos will change it."

"And it's the hardest truth to learn," added Jenny.

What Vince said then, I cannot repeat, because no one would publish it. Finally he shouted, "I'll get even with the lot of you," and went out, slamming the door after him.

Jenny was sitting with her head in her hands, when Bill came in. "Can I sit down?" he asked. "I've got bad news to impart."

"Not now, not this minute," Jenny said. "I can't face any more problems just now."

"It won't keep," Bill replied pulling out his stool and sitting on it before saying, "Alice has gone."

"Gone? Gone where?" asked Jenny looking up.

"She's dead," he said with dreadful finality. "Didn't show up for Christmas dinner and was found dead in her chair. She had a heart attack."

There was a long mind-bending silence before Josh said," "It was a good way to go." And I asked, "Was she very old?"

"Eighty two. She didn't let me tell you. 'If they know how old I am, they won't want me, Bill,' she said. Those were her very words. She didn't like being old you know, hated it. But at least she didn't suffer in the end," said Bill.

I did not want to hear any more. I went out into the yard and talked to Fantasy, who rubbed his head on me, and I thought, 'Alice will never be here again. It's over.' And then the tears came, not just for Alice but because we all die in the end, and there's nothing one can do about it, not yet anyway. (Josh, who is good at science, says it will change with time). Then I thought, thank goodness Josh and I cared enough to visit her and she was eighty two and that is really old, and as Josh said, it was a good way to go. But I still went on crying until Josh appeared and, putting his arm around me, said, "She had a good life, and she kept going to the end. Think of the people who die in wars and accidents, young and full of life, think of them, Cathy. It's not a tragedy, so do cheer up. You know she wouldn't want you to cry."

"But she was poor and alone, there was no one there," I replied wiping my eyes. "And we never really appreciated her, did we? I mean she helped so much. I miss her all the time already. I keep seeing her pushing a wheelbarrow across the yard, and I was so impatient with her sometimes. I was really foul."

But Josh said that Alice would have understood and that life had to go on, and then Jenny appeared and told us that the funeral was on Tuesday and that we would have to attend, and that Alice's niece, who was quite old herself, was managing everything, and that Alice had asked for donations for Horsehaven instead of flowers.

"There you are," I said, "She was so poor but she thought of us right to the very end."

"Oh Cathy stop being so pathetic," said Josh crossly. "You know we all have to die and she was eighty two."

I had never been to a funeral before. Jenny said that my school clothes would do and that I need not dress up and certainly not in black. She said that Alice would have wanted smiling faces and that it was to be a celebration of her life, not a vigil.

There were not many people at Alice's funeral. Gillian and Sarah came and cried all through the service. Bill came and a few neighbours from Treadmill, and some strangers who must have been relations, two of them smelling of expensive perfume, arrived in a huge Mercedes. The hymns were cheerful ones including *All Things Bright and Beautiful*, and Jenny climbed into the pulpit to say how she remembered Alice and Josh did the same, looking brilliant with his fair hair shining. He said how much she had helped us and how much we had grown to love her during the short time we had known her. We were each given a single flower by Jenny to throw on to Alice's coffin as it lay in its newly dug grave. As I threw mine I thought, 'death puts everything in perspective, because compared to it, our problems are trivial.' Alice's niece had arranged a small reception at Rose Cottage and we went there after the funeral.

There were lots of tiny sandwiches and tea and the couple who had come in the Mercedes talked about Alice in loud, uncaring voices.

"Of course she was quite dotty at the end; all she cared about was horses, she had them on the brain," said the woman laughing, before fingering Alice's ornaments and saying things like, "This could be worth quite a lot of money."

Josh and I didn't stay long at the reception. We thanked the niece, who wore her grey hair piled on top of her head in an old fashioned way, for having us, before we set off on foot for Horsehaven.

"That was what is called a funeral breakfast," said Josh. "In other countries they hold a feast."

"I didn't feel like eating," I replied as we ran down a road, then took a footpath across frozen fields. "Vicky will be going mad," I continued climbing a stile. "She's been shut up for hours."

"So will the horses because it's long past feed time," replied Josh.

The hymns were still echoing in my head; somehow the service had made me feel better so that now it was over, I felt tempted to give joyful bucks like a horse just turned out into a field after a long time stabled.

Soon we could see our wood and then we saw something which made us stop in our tracks before crying out, "Look, look at the smoke," in unison.

Everything fled from my mind at that moment, everything but the smoke billowing across our fields, acrid clouds of it; then we were both running, while my heart cried and my mind saw dying horses - Trooper, Fantasy, Morag, Rocky,

Kelpie, huge noble Torchy - for thinking we might be late back we had put them in their loose boxes for the night before leaving for Alice's funeral.

Never had I run so fast before; but Josh was way ahead as we neared the stables. He stopped only once to call over his shoulder, "It's the hay. The fire hasn't reached the stables yet."

As we arrived, a fire engine roared into the yard, siren wailing. "Josh, help me get the horses out," I shouted.

As the firemen trained their hoses onto the hay, another fire engine arrived, then another. The yard was full of smoke, different blacker smoke than before. I found headcollars and led out Trooper, turned him into a field before a fireman called, "It's all right, the fire's under control, it won't reach the stables now."

And it was true, the fire was dying down already, but the damage was done for though not all the hay was burnt, all of it was ruined.

"We're just damping down," a fireman said after a while.

We fetched them mugs of tea. A lad had rung the Station, one said, he had sounded agitated. He had called from a phone box, said another.

I knew who it was then - Vince! It had to be. Vince had set fire to our hay and then, afraid that the fire would kill the horses, rung the fire brigade. It all fitted. I found Vicky hiding under a chair in the sitting room. Someone had been in my room, pulled my drawers open and smashed my china horses. But by now I was too devastated for tears.

Josh looked at me and said, "Cathy, it's not your

fault. Vince can't make you like him. He's just so
thick and altogether yuk."

"I'll have to go away," I said slowly.

But Josh replied that now I was being silly and
that it was probably Vince's final fling. And that
he would be sent away to a detention centre. Josh
insisted that I was over-reacting as usual. "I expect he's on cocaine or something stupid like that,"
he finished, as Jenny appeared in the Land Rover
sounding the horn and shouting, "Is it the hay? Is
it all gone?"

At six o'clock the firemen went home. The horses
waited in their stables to be fed, whinnying and
knocking on their doors. Torchy stared at Josh with
appealing eyes, asking why there was no hay net
hanging in his box.

It was almost dark now and we had no hay to
give any of them. "We're finished," Jenny said
staring at the blackened hay. "This is the last straw
literally; it's the absolute end."

"I'll ring all the local farmers and see whether
we can fetch some hay in the Land Rover. I've got
£10 at home," Josh said ignoring, Jenny's remark.
"Dad sent it to me for Christmas and I don't want
it."

"That will buy three bales of hay, just enough for
tonight if we give the animals three quarter
rations, but what about tomorrow and the day
after? And the day after that? What about January,
February, March and most of April?" Jenny asked
staring into space. "How could Vince do this to us?
How could he, when I put up with him all over
Christmas and even gave him a present I couldn't

afford? I was sorry for him because I know what it's like to be rejected and I thought he needed help. And now he's done this to us. How could he, the snivelling rat?"

"Remember when he let out the horses?" I asked.

"Of course I do," snapped Jenny. "But I forgave him because I thought he needed help and had had a rotten life. What a fool I am!"

"Some people are born rotten," Josh said. "Look, I'll go home and get my money and maybe, if Mum's in a good mood, she'll give me a bit more."

But at that moment a tractor appeared, pulling a flat trailer loaded with hay. "I thought you might need this," called a burly man. "We heard about your fire on the local news and I said to my wife, 'how are they going to feed their rescued animals now?' It's only fifty bales, I couldn't spare any more," he continued, getting down from his tractor, "And there are a few bales of straw on the back. I don't want any money for it. It's a gift like, just to see you through. I hope you were insured. My barns were set on fire last year so I know what you are going through. Cheer up," he continued patting Jenny on the shoulder. "When my barn went up in smoke, I lost half my herd of Jerseys too. You get over it, you have to."

We unloaded the hay into an empty loose box. Jenny was completely silent now, her small face tear-stained and tight with emotion. She was cracking up; any fool could see that.

She fetched the farmer, who was called Martin Tring, a glass of beer and we all thanked him profusely. He downed the beer before he said, "I don't know where you'll get any more hay; it's in short supply this year. It was the dry spring which did it." They were killing words, which hung suspended like a death sentence in the cold air. "And it looks as though we're in for a hard winter," he continued climbing heavily onto his tractor.

We shouted our thanks as he drove away, then rushed to the loose box to fill hay nets full of the hay he had brought, which smelt like hay should, sweet and clean.

"Jenny's got a death wish for Horsehaven," Josh muttered to me. "I don't know what we're going to do about it."

"Nor do I."

"But we must do something."

"But what?" I asked.

The horses had feared the worst and now their eyes lit up as they saw me bringing them hay; and they whinnied ecstatically.

"She'll sell the wood. It's a foregone conclusion," I called, feeding Trooper.

"That's better than selling the place," Josh replied, feeding Torchy.

"And there's no way out. We owe too much money now," I said.

"There's the donations from Alice's funeral in lieu of flowers," replied Josh.

"But there was hardly anyone there," I answered. "And don't think that posh couple will send any money. They don't even like horses."

"Stop it, your gloom is making me feel sick," Josh replied. "I don't want to think about our troubles any more. I'm going to Africa in the summer to see my Dad. I may not return. So it doesn't matter so much for me. It's you and the horses I'm thinking of and all the ones which will never be rescued now."

We were pushing a wheelbarrow of hay to the fields now. Everything was white and crisp with frost. There was a pale, cold moon in the night sky which cast a cold vivid light.

"It's been a terrible week; even Christmas was gloomy this year. We must be growing up," I said. "Do you think you ever grow out of Christmas?"

"It changes, that's what I think," replied Josh, opening a field gate.

Josh's mother fetched him that evening, saying that it was too cold for him to cycle home and that the roads were sheets of ice. Watching him go I thought, he's going to Africa, he may stay. If Horsehaven is no more, he probably will. And I thought life is all goodbyes, first to Alice for ever, and soon to Josh. And now I felt very cold.

"There's some supper in the simmering oven and I've put a hot water bottle in your bed. Don't bother to wash up." It was only seven thirty but Jenny was in her dressing gown already.

I fed Vicky. "Something will turn up," I suggested.

"If you say that again, I'll scream," replied Jenny, not meaning it of course, just expressing her despair. "And I've made up my mind, I am selling the wood, there's no other way, Cathy, and don't look at me like that. I don't want to do it. You're not the only one who loves it."

# CHAPTER TEN

## "THEY WON'T NEED ME ANY MORE"

That night I dreamt that Vince was standing over my bed holding a knife.

"I'm going to tattoo you," he said. "I'm going to put my name on your arm; then everyone will know you are mine." I woke up shivering all over. It was morning. Jenny was talking to Charles on the telephone, wearing her dressing gown again.

Later that day the police arrived and took statements from us. My mind was still living my terrible dream. I think we all looked shattered, even Josh who arrived presently on his bike with a scarf covering half his face. Light snow was falling now, slowly invading the yard like an enemy.

I think we all blamed Vince for the fire. The police knew him. When he had let out all our horses he had received community service as a punishment. This time he would be put away, a policeman said, standing in the tack room, adding that he remembered the smell of saddle soap from when he was a boy and worked in racing stables one long hot summer. A policewoman accompanied the policeman and I told her about the tattoo on Vince's arm, and said that really the whole incident was my fault, because I hadn't dealt with Vince sensibly and had lost my temper, which anyone who has anything to do with horses, knows they should never do. I cannot remember how she answered, but I know what she said succeeded in driving the last remnants of the hideous dream from my mind.

After the police had gone, I took Vicky for a walk and said goodbye to the trees in our wood one by one. Returning, I found Josh sitting with his head in his hands on a box in the tack room. A large, nearly new Volvo was parked in the yard. "There's a man in the house with Jenny; he's either a bank manager or a developer. He's wearing a suit and is grey-haired," Josh said. "I think it's the end of Horsehaven." He stared at me with his incredibly blue eyes, before adding, "I think we are going to sell the horses to pay our debts."

"Not the rescued ones," I cried. "We can't."

"No, not them, the ones Jenny had for the riding school, the ones she rescued before we became a registered charity - Fantasy, Trooper, Squid and Fidget. I expect the others will go to other charities or be put down." I had never seen Josh so gloomy before.

"If we go into liquidation, she'll have to sell up; it's the law," he said, standing up. "And you can't tangle with it. So get your skates on, Cathy, and think of what you're going to do next. You know Mark and his mother are both trustees," he went on in the same toneless voice, a voice I had never heard before. "Mark and his mother, I ask you?"

"What can I do? I only have a little money in my account, and anyway my account book's lost," I answered glumly.

"Find it and we'll buy some hay with what you've

116

got, and I will add my money to it. Okay? We won't give up yet. We'll get your modelling going again. We'll have another Open Day," said Josh. "We'll make our parents trustees." But I don't think he believed what he was saying because he still looked like a beaten dog.

We walked round the horses with mad ideas going round and round in our heads, ideas we knew deep down would never come to anything. We watched Jenny's caller, coming out of the house carrying a brief case, before waving cheerfully to us and getting into his car and driving away. Josh called him a name I won't repeat, before we looked at each other again and Josh said, "If she's come to some dreadful deal, there's nothing we can do," and I thought of the summer coming and that Josh would be in Africa, but where would I be with no Horsehaven? And I thought, our money is just chicken feed compared to what we need. And I thought, we're in a long dark tunnel and there's no way out.

Then together we peered through the kitchen window. Jenny was talking to someone on the telephone, gesticulating with her hands, sounding quite merry. "She's had a death wish about this place for some time; now it's finished she's happy," said Josh bitterly.

"It's Charles. He says he's horsey, but he's not like us and Alice. He's always been on the fringe hasn't he?" I asked.

"Yet he must be quite rich because he drives a good car, so why can't he bale us out?" demanded Josh, looking round the yard with an anguished expression.

"Perhaps Jenny won't let him." Vicky looked at me with sad eyes; she was blaming herself for my misery, wondering what she had done wrong. The Jenny opened the door to call, "Come in. I've got things to tell you. I've summoned Gillian and Sarah because it affects us all."

And Josh said, "She's winding us up. She's going to offer you Trooper and me Torchy, and you have nowhere to keep a horse and I'm going to Africa."

"Coffee or tea?" offered Jenny as we went inside.

There were lots of sheets of paper on the kitchen table as well as accounts which had not been paid, final demands, threats, all the things you get when you can't pay bills. I had seen them all before when Dad was out of work, only they weren't vets' bills then; but loans at exorbitant rates, and mortgage repayments my parents were unable to settle. The misery of it all came back to me now.

"Biscuits?" said Jenny passing round a tin. Josh and I shook our heads. Neither of us felt like eating. Climbing onto my knee, Vicky licked my ear; she was losing her puppy smell and was nearly as big as a spaniel now, but she didn't have a spaniel's ears. Her tail was feathery, her white waistcoat like satin. Mostly she spoke to me with her eyes, which had two dear little pale blobs above them.

"Some good news. Cynthia has just rung me. She wants a modelling session by the sea. I suggested Westcliffe-on-Sea. She's ringing your father about advertising his site at the same time. The catalogue's going worldwide. We've decided to use

Torchy this time, Tommy and Morag and the foals. She's hiring a horse box," Jenny said. "We will be waiting for the right weather though. We must have sunshine, because the clothes are for the Spring and Summer," she continued. I looked out of the window; snow was falling, snow on snow. I didn't want to think about modelling clothes. Once it had seemed so important, but not any more.

"You'll have to get your hair done Cathy," Jenny went on. "And here's your Building Society book. I had it in my desk all the time, because I didn't want you spending your money on Horsehaven. Here, take it."

I snatched it, rudely. "You might have told me. I've looked and looked for it. I even blamed poor Vicky for eating it. I can't think how you could be so mean; I had nightmares about it," I cried furiously.

At that moment Charles came in, dressed casually for once. He stopped to smile at us all, before getting himself a mug of coffee. Then he stooped to kiss Jenny on the cheek. "Is this some sort of conference? I mean, what is going on?" demanded Josh. "We can't stay in here for hours doing nothing; there are things which need doing outside."

"Exactly," I agreed disagreeably.

"Calm down," replied Jenny. "All will be revealed in a few minutes; we're just waiting for Gillian and Sarah."

"What have they got to do with anything? They're not helpers any more," replied Josh angrily.

I could hear Torchy banging on his loose box door.

We were already late with his feed, and horses hate meals being late. We all knew that. Jenny once said that they had clocks in their heads. But that was a long time ago, before liquidation hung over us like a black cloud.

Gillian and Sarah came in. "Mum's gone away to shop. She says she will be back in forty minutes. Is that all right?" asked Gillian, who had grown and was nearly as tall as me now, while Sarah seemed just the same, with the same elfin face and with her long hair still tied back.

Charles fetched them both coffee. Josh looked at his watch and sighed. Outside the snow was falling faster, and it didn't look like stopping.

When we were all sitting down, Jenny said, "It's to do with Alice. Except for a few legacies she's left all her money to Horsehaven."

"But it can't be much, because she was so poor," I said after a moment. "We all know that. She bought all her clothes at charity shops, and only had a one bar electric fire in her sitting room."

"I suppose it will pay for some hay, but it won't help much, because her car was twenty years old and all rusty," agreed Josh, sounding bemused.

"She did think she was poor. Her husband died twenty years ago and she hardly spent any money afterwards. She sold her big house and came to Treadmill to save money. It's an incredible story," continued Jenny.

All of a sudden I felt very cold. I saw Alice in my imagination in her old coat pushing a barrow across the yard, her tangled grey hair, her worn hands, her cheap darned gloves. I saw her warming her little tin of Kaolin in an old saucepan on the stove. I saw her lancing Trooper's abscess and being sweet to Vicky. Suddenly I wanted to burst into tears.

"In fact she was worth over a million and she's left it all to Horsehaven, except for the legacies I've just mentioned," continued Jenny looking at us each in turn. "Well, what do you say?"

"Brilliant," cried Josh. "Now we can get on with the feeding." And I knew that Jenny's remarks had still to sink into his head.

"Don't you want to hear about the legacies? Well, I'll tell you anyway. Alice has left £3,000 to you Cathy and the same to you Josh, and some to me and £500 each to Gillian and Sarah. She wrote that you were always sweet to an old lady and a lot more besides," said Jenny. "Now we can celebrate. Or are you all too thick to understand a word of what I've just said?"

It's true, I could not take in what Jenny had said. It was such a shock and I was trying to see Alice in a completely new light, not as a poor little old lady, but a rich one. I looked at the snow still falling outside. The horses still had to be fed. And I knew if I mentioned it Josh would say that I was being a martyr again.

"It won't hurt the horses to wait ten minutes, Cathy. They are all in and we have got electricity," said Jenny, reading my thoughts and laughing. "And now we can have their teeth done, and we can build a new office and appoint new trustees. We can even have a permanent paid helper. We are all right. We needn't sell the wood. Good old

121

Alice," cried Jenny. "And another thing, Charles and I are going to get married."

I was incapable of digesting so much. Everything seemed to be changing before my eyes. My whole purpose in life was vanishing. Did I need to model clothes on a cold beach if we were now so rich? If we were having a paid helper, was I needed any more? If Charles and Jenny were getting married would they want me to go on living in my room? Suddenly I realised that being rich can destroy things just as drastically as being poor. The air in the kitchen was full of celebration; Alice would have wanted it that way and after all Jenny was going to marry Charles, whom I had been told had two nearly grown up children and was divorced. So there was more than one thing to celebrate. But I was still unable to join in. "I'm going outside to feed the horses," I cried. "Oh don't be a martyr, Cathy," said Josh as I stood up, before rushing outside with Vicky at my heels, my mind in turmoil. The horses whinnied, when they saw me and Torchy started to bang on his door. They were my friends; they never changed. Fantasy stared at me, his thin neck a little fatter at last, his lop ears looking as ridiculous as ever. Trooper nickered politely. None of them yelled at me for being late, or said that my hair was full of hay, or needed cutting.

Then Josh appeared. "For goodness sake, Cathy, don't spoil everything. This is the moment when all our dreams have come true," he cried.

I remembered my English teacher quoting once: "To travel hopefully is a better thing than to

arrive." It is by Robert Louis Stevenson and I
quoted it now. "They won't need me any more. Can't
you see? Or are you blind?" I cried.

"Of course they will. Anyway we all move on. You
don't want to be still here when you are an old
lady like Alice, do you?" asked Josh. We finished
feeding the stabled horses. It was still snowing.
"The paid helper they get will be ill sometimes
and then you will be needed. And what about when
Charles and Jenny go on their honeymoon, you
will be needed then," Josh said. "You will have time
to pass your GCSEs now and there isn't much time
left. You don't want to be always poor, or unem-
ployed for the rest of your life, do you? Though
you could be a model," Josh finished laughing.

I knew he was right - Alice dying, Jenny getting
married, suddenly being better off was all part of
life. And Jenny needed Charles; with him she
would be safe.

"You should go on a holiday, see the world. This
is such a tiny part of it. When I'm in Africa I shall
think of you pushing a wheelbarrow across the
yard. The same old Cathy," said Josh, as we took
hay to Squid and Fidget, who were living out at
last. Our footprints left fresh imprints in the snow.
And now at last I could see myself moving on, buying my own horse, qualifying in horse psychology,
becoming famous.

"What are you going to spend your £3,000 on?"
Josh asked as we turned back to the stables.

"Some new boots," I said. "I really can't think of
anything else I want, though I might buy a new
rug for Trooper."

123

"I'll bring you back a present from Africa," said Josh. We stood in the snow, seeing the years ahead. "I shall keep most of my dosh to help see me through college. I think I have to train for eight years to be a vet, and then it's a life sentence of hard work," continued Josh. "And I intend to be a horse specialist."

I saw him grown up, wearing a white coat with a stethoscope round his neck. He would look fantastic. Even when his hair was grey, he would still look fantastic. One day we'll meet again and fall really in love. We will both have jobs by then, real jobs, but the last few days will be the ones I will always remember, I thought.

"We won't have to worry about Horsehaven ever again will we now?" I asked. "The barns can always be full of hay and the bins full of feed and the vets will come whenever we want them."

"And we won't have to muck out loose box after loose box ever again; sell on Open Days, and bus loads of visitors will come here, so many that there will be a special car park for them and proper toilets," cried Josh and suddenly we were both laughing.

"We will get a horsebox which will take five horses and build an isolation block, so that we never ever get strangles again," I cried.

"We'll be trustees ourselves and arrange things the way we want them," cried Josh. "We'll sit in on committees. We'll have our names on the notepaper which will have Fantasy's head on it, lop ears and all."

"And a monthly mag for our supporters called

HORSEHAVEN with Trooper's head on it," I added laughing more than ever.

"And one day I'll be in charge of the horses' health and you of their minds, Cathy," said Josh, suddenly serious again. We were now so carried away that neither of us felt the snow falling on our bare heads, faster and faster.

We returned to the kitchen and Jenny told us that Vince had been taken into custody, accused of arson. "That will keep him out of your hair for a bit, Cathy," she added laughing. "And by the way, another bit of news you may or may not like, Charles and I are really getting married in April and you are all invited. I know it's quite soon, but we are both getting older all the time."

I saw now that all the terrible lines of worry had left Jenny's face. I hugged her. "Congratulations, I should have said it before but I was too surprised. And you don't look old at all Jenny, you look great, you always do."

"It will be a simple wedding with a blessing in church," Jenny went on. "I think everything will be easier with Charles helping, at least he can add two and two together." And she laughed again.

Gillian and Sarah's mother arrived and after hearing all the wonderful news and kissing Jenny, took them home.

Then I telephoned Mum. "Guess what?" I cried. "We're going to be all right. We're never ever going to be short of money again." I don't think she took in what I said because she only replied, "A letter has arrived from your school Cath complaining about your attendance and lack of endeavour -

whatever that means. Your Dad's really upset. The point is you're not stupid, you could do much, much better, that's what the letter says. You're wasting the best years of your life, Cath, cleaning up after horses which aren't even yours."

"But I will do better now Mum, because I shan't have to get up early and muck out any more; we are going to have full time help," I replied, "So in the evenings I shall concentrate on my school work. And if Jenny's ill, there will be the full time helper to do the work. I want to pass my GCSEs, Mum, I really do. And it hasn't been a waste of time working here because when I'm older I want to become a horse psychologist."

I don't think Mum took in a word of what I said. She sighed and told me that there was a sixth form college opening at Westcliffe-on-Sea in the autumn. "But you're not going to make the grade Cath, that's what your teacher says; not the way you're going."

"Josh will help me. He's brilliant," I argued and at the same time saw myself attending a brand new college, making new friends, moving on, but knew at the same time that Horsehaven would remain part of me for ever, that I would never give up loving it, whatever happened. And then I thought, if I move to Westcliffe-on-Sea I'll be safe from Vince, because Dad will see him off. "I've been left some money too, Mum, a lot. But I'm never giving up Horsehaven completely," I continued. "It's just that with Charles and Jenny getting married, I think they may want my room back. But I shall keep returning and I'll still love

Fantasy's head grey with age and Trooper's too.

Mum didn't seem to be taking anything in for she sighed again and said, "Well it will be lovely to have you back one day Cath, you don't know how we miss you. And Vicky of course," she added as an afterthought.

"I mean it. I am going to live at home again," I said before I put down the receiver, thinking at the same time that Horsehaven was my real home and had been for several years and nothing could alter that. But that one had to move on; grow up, change.

When I eventually went to bed that night I lay for hours awake looking back at what we had achieved. Mum had said that I was wasting my time, but I knew that wasn't true. Our horses and ponies were living proof of that, and they deserved a good life, every one of them. Then I thought how lovely it would be to lie in bed on cold winter mornings listening to someone else pushing a wheelbarrow across the frozen yard, not Alice, but someone young and strong; someone I could turn to when Jenny was out and everything in chaos. And now in spite of the cold, I felt warm and safe as I imagined the beech trees still in the wood year after year and Horsehaven becoming famous. I knew then whatever happened, the last few years had been worthwhile; and no one could take that away from me for it was already history. And before I slept I resolved never to worry so much ever again about anything.